#3

For Martha

What is the past, after all, but a vast sheet of darkness in which a few moments, pricked apparently at random, shine?
John Updike

GRANDFATHER

Chapter 1

In the early morning hours of July 24, 1915, the crew of the Great Lakes excursion steamer S.S. *Eastland* prepared for that morning's journey. They hauled in the steamer's gangplank, forcing a latecomer to leap aboard from the wharf along the Chicago River. Despite the cool, damp weather, 2,573 passengers and crew were already aboard the *Eastland*; the atmosphere was one big party.

As the *Eastland* completed loading its passengers, it began to list to port, away from the wharf. The movement didn't alarm the partygoers, but it alarmed many dockworkers.

Then, it listed even farther to port. Water poured through the open gangways into the engine room. The crew stood there in horror as the water level climbed up their pants. The men then scrambled up a ladder to the main deck.

At 7:29 a.m., the *Eastland* listed to a 45-degree angle. The buffet on the restaurant deck rolled to the port wall, almost crushing two women; a freezer followed, pinning a woman beneath it. Water rushed into open portholes in the cabins below deck. The deadliest shipwreck in Great Lakes history—a calamity that would take more passenger lives than the sinking of the *Titanic* or the *Lusitania*—was underway. Within minutes after it listed 45 degrees to port, it rolled over.

When the boat keeled over, people on the upper deck were hurled off like a dog shaking water from its fur. In an instant, the river was black with struggling, crying, frightened, drowning humanity. Children bobbed about like corks. Many of those who knew how to swim made it to shore only ten yards away. Those who didn't swim, soon disappeared underwater.

By 7:30 a.m., the *Eastland* was lying on its side in 20 feet of murky water, still tied to the dock. The vessel had toppled so quickly, there was no time to launch the lifesaving equipment. As the *Eastland* bobbed on its side, many passengers simply climbed over the starboard railing and walked across the exposed hull to safety, never even getting their feet wet. The *Eastland's* captain was one of them.

They were among the lucky ones.

10,000 people were wandering about the riverfront that day—grocery and poultry merchants, their customers, Western Electric workers waiting to board other ships, dozens of other trades and merchants. Onlookers leaped into action. Some jumped into the river and began saving lives. Others threw whatever might float into the water, including pallets of lumber and wooden chicken crates. Some of the pallets struck passengers in the water, knocking them out and putting them under. Parents clutched children and disappeared together beneath the brown water or lost their grip and watched their children sink out of sight. "God, the screaming was terrible. It's ringing in my ears yet," a warehouse worker told a reporter.

* * *

Two blocks away, seventeen-year-old Knowles Gresham looked out past his Cyclone's handlebars at the Chicago skyline. Moving ever nearer, thunderheads heaved and tore the sky apart. He could smell the summer rain, so he decided to stop, nurse a sandwich and coffee, and wait out the coming squall. He turned onto River Street.

The Cyclone motorcycle's straight pipes reverberated against the skyscrapers and lesser buildings. After coming upright out of the turn, Knowles leaned back and relaxed. He smiled at the music of the V-Twin 45 horsepower engine. The throttle rapped for the far-off seagulls until they danced like kites. He laughed, another great day on two wheels.

A block south, at the stop sign just before the bridge, Knowles's feet went down to the pavement. As he waited for the light, he noticed other drivers seemed to have forgotten all traffic rules: the intersection was jammed with cars and trucks and horse-drawn wagons honking and beeping and inching forward, pulling around, trying to get through the horrendous mess. A bluecoat policeman came running up to Knowles. "Can you swim?"

"I can."

"Come with me. We've hundreds of people drowning!"

Knowles followed the copper on his Cyclone. He heard the screaming crescendo when he pulled off his leather helmet and goggles. Finally crossing the bridge, he drove his bike up onto the sidewalk and parked. "People were struggling in the water, clustered so thickly that they covered the surface of the river," he would recall. "The screaming was the most horrible of all."

Knowles slid down the bank and scrambled onto the *Eastland's* hull. He saw passengers cut and bleeding. He dove in and began dragging people to the bank where reaching hands pulled them up out of the water.

Thirty minutes later, Knowles, cramping in the cold water, decided it was time to warm up, so out he came. Upon making the top of the riverbank, Knowles directed a hospital employee to telephone Marshall Field & Company, the department store, for 500 blankets. Then he found a local phone box and called restaurants, asking for hot soup and coffee to be delivered to the scene.

As survivors made it to the dock, Knowles decided to send the less injured home. He would later tell his uncle that he merely went out into the street, stopped the first automobile that came along, loaded it up with people, and told the owner or driver where to take them. Not one driver said no.

By 8 a.m., almost all the survivors were pulled from the river. Then came the gruesome task of locating and removing bodies.

The crowding and confusion were terrible. Rescuers, emergency personnel, and curious onlookers flocked to the scene. By noon, divers and rescue workers finally reached bodies that had been trapped underwater in the port-side cabins. The complexion of those recovered changed now: it was all women and children.

Several priests arrived. They were there to hear confessions but for the most part, ended up performing last rites. Even they were white-faced and stunned, many streaming tears down their cheeks.

Stretcher-bearers traversed the hull as bodies were lifted out. "I wondered dully why they waited for stretchers at all," wrote Gretchen Krohn in the *New York Times*. "All the bodies carried past were so rigid that poles to carry them by seemed superfluous; and the pitiful shortness of most of them." She continued, "Sometimes, the dead clung so tightly to one another that they were loaded in twos onto single stretchers. There was quickly a shortage of ambulances, so American Express trucks were called curbside to transport bodies."

Knowles, somewhat warmed from his ten minutes ashore, went back into the water and resumed his lifesaving assistance.

Chapter 2

By 1:30, the weeping survivors were all back onshore. Some among them were ravenously devouring burgers and downing hot coffee donated from restaurants all around. They walked amongst the dead while holding out hope their loved ones were merely missing rather than lying covered in a sheet along the sidewalk, stacked like cordwood.

After the *Eastland* rolled, 844 passengers died on that lazy urban river, 20 feet from the dock.

Shortly after the last body was pulled ashore, Knowles climbed out of the river, exhausted and shaking from the icy water. While he craved hot coffee and food, he left what food and drink that was still available, to the survivors themselves. They needed it more than anyone else.

All around, the curbsides and parking lots were full. He stepped between and around vehicles as he made his way to his motorcycle. The kick-starter caught, and then he edged into bumper-to-bumper traffic. Riding slowly, mostly dragging his feet on the pavement, he putted two blocks down to a restaurant that appeared to be open for business. His body was crying out for warmth. He parked his bike beneath the front window and stepped inside the cafe.

The restaurant was loud but quite warm. There must have been two dozen conversations competing to be heard. Flatware jangled in the bus boys' trays.

Just like he predicted, the air was thick with the smell of burnt eggs and greasy hamburgers. All tables and booths were crammed. Everybody was watching everybody else as if waiting for an announcement that the tragedy two blocks south was in fact just a mirage. But the announcement never came.

Moving from front to rear, looking for an empty table, he didn't see the one short, round man seated off to his left. The man worked with his fork and a dinner roll at the fatty steak and potatoes on his plate. His eyes remained downcast as he devoured his lunch. He said nothing to anyone, no smiles at the baby in the next booth, no refill requests to the wandering waitress with the stained coffee pot. His name was Alphonse Capone.

Knowles walked by the man, beelining for the one empty stool at the counter.

As he passed, a booth of cops turned to study him. Knowles shook his head and allowed a small smile. Where he had been a hero just ten minutes before, now he was a suspect since he'd arrived on a motorcycle. It was the same everywhere: A few cops hated bikers, and some bikers hated cops. And those same cops toyed with bikers when they were alone and most vulnerable. The ones at the table rolled their eyes and shrugged, trading a look among themselves, before returning to their small talk.

The stool placed the cops at his back. Which was fine. The waitress behind the counter glanced his way. Knowles's handsome face made the corners of her mouth turn up. He was still youthful, chasing just eighteen years of age, and she liked what she saw. The cops witnessed the moment and scowled. Heads shook in disgust.

Knowles folded his hands and waited.

Waitresses scurried back and forth like soldiers defending their wall from starving invaders. He smiled; it was always the same at every Chicago eatery—hunger, followed by hot food, followed by a green slip, followed by dollar bills.

Finally, the red-haired one stopped across from him. After she popped her gum, she moistened the pencil lead on the tip of her tongue while she stared at him and waited. She did not attempt to hide it from anyone who might be watching: she was interested. The cops nudged each other. One of them threatened to confront the biker and ask to see his driver's license. But the restaurant was no place for that. They stayed in their seats.

"Fries and burger, medium well."

"Hon, there ain't no medium nothing in here. Everything's burned just the same."

He nodded. "I can do that."

She made a mark on her order pad and stepped closer. "Couldn't help but notice that belt. That real turquoise?"

"It is."

"Where from?"

"Navajo reservation. My mother was there. The kachina on my buckle"—he stood and pulled outward on the belt to show her—"is a Navajo spirit. Not a holy one like the Hopis. But this guy is used in healing ceremonies."

"Lift your jacket and turn around."

"No, I'm tired and wet. Let me have my coffee, please."

She ignored his response. "How many conchos?" she asked.

"Eight." Now he stood and lifted his wet T-shirt so she could count the round, sterling silver decorative buttons riveted to the belt.

She whistled appreciatively. "Nice. Like the tight jeans, too. What's your name, hon?"

"Knowles."

He sat back down. He didn't pay any attention to the cops. But they paid attention to him. They'd watched the belt show-and-tell and then turned to roll eyes at each other. They shook their heads. One city cop, the largest and youngest of the four officers, nodded. It was on.

Red returned in five minutes with his order. "Gonna be around long?" she asked. She wasn't embarrassed by the implication of her question.

"Naw. Headed home. Up north."

"Evanston?"

He didn't reply, instead taking a massive bite of the sandwich.

She watched him chew. "That burnt enough for you?"

"It'll do. Are we out of ketchup?"

She moved to the back counter and returned with a red bottle. "Help yo-self, Big Time."

"No big time here. Small change is all."

"If you say so, sugar, if you say so. Be right back."

She stepped around the counter and went behind Knowles, having been summoned to the booth where the cops were finishing up.

"Who's Rapid Roy?" asked the largest cop.

The waitress retorted, "Who's asking, Ralphie?" She punched the cop playfully in the shoulder, and he feinted as if kicked by a mule.

"Me, that's who," said the cop. "Who is he?"

"Some guy passing through. He is soaking wet. My guess is he pulled people to safety today. My guess is he saved lives. Did you, Ralphie? And why do you ask?"

"Just watching the fashion show. Was it you asked to see his ass?"

She shook her head in disgust. "It wasn't the ass—though that wasn't bad, either. It's the belt he's wearing. That thing set him back at least twenty bucks from where I'm sitting."

"Twenty bucks! Holy—"

"Yes, and you assholes leave him alone when he leaves. He wasn't showing off. He was showing me the damn belt. We okay?"

"We are if you are, sugar," said the deputy across from the cop.

The law enforcement officers smiled gleefully, their eyes glittering with anticipation.

Knowles chewed his burger and washed it down with coffee. He wiped his mouth with a napkin when he was finished and worked at the grease on his fingers. He pulled another napkin from the dispenser and repeated. Red came by. She scribbled on her pad then laid a green ticket before him. She had drawn a heart with an arrow through it. Her name and phone number were off to the side. *Call me if you want,* she had written underneath. He smiled and pushed up from the stool. The cops were gone by the time he approached the cashier. He paid with a one, returned to his seat, and plopped down the extra coins for the redhead. She wasn't around. He lumbered off, then walked outside.

* * *

The rainstorm had blown through, leaving the street puddled. He stretched. Overhead, the sun was shining, He cupped his hand over his eyes, looking east. He could make out a squall line across the eastern sky, black and slanted.

Knowles threw his leg over the bike, pulled the machine upright, and kicked back the side stand. The kick-starter caught instantly as it should. The bike was a 1915 model with less than a grand on the dial. As he walked it back from the curb, he turned the handlebars. The motorcycle came around, and he dropped it into first gear and putted away from the river, onto the asphalt heading east. Nothing illegal, lights all working, no tailgating, no antics to bother anyone. Pure joy.

Four blocks down the road, he was passing by Marshall Fields, when he saw it—a single flash in the left-hand mirror. Then both mirrors filled with red flashing lights. A hulking figure behind the wheel of a police car was hunched forward, maybe smiling, too far away to know for sure.

Knowles came down off a bridge, slowed, and pulled into the parking lane. He turned to watch the cop approach. He smiled pleasantly at the man.

Up beside him strode the youngest cop from the cafe, cocksure and frowning. He looked to be ten years older than Knowles—maybe twenty-seven. In his uniform and hat, he stood six-two. He thrust his chest forward and rested his hand on his holster. His fingers toyed with the strap release.

"You got a gun, boy?" were his first words to Knowles.

"No, officer. Look, I—"

"Whoa up, Nellie. You'll speak when I ask you. Let's get that up front. Roger that?"

"Roger," said Knowles.

"All right, climb off that iron and lead us back to my squad. Place both hands on the hood."

Knowles did as ordered. He thought it odd that he would be frisked for what should only have been a minor traffic stop. So minor, in fact, that he was clueless why he'd been pulled over.

"Any knives or needles? Anything that might cut me or jab me?"

"No, sir."

"If you're lying, it's your ass, boy."

He came up behind Knowles and patted him down. Then he stood upright and began thrusting his hands into Knowles's pants pockets. He removed Knowles's wallet, money clip, and loose change—all soaked. There was nothing else. He reached around and unclasped Knowles's belt buckle. With one hand, he pulled the belt from its loops as one would whip a long snake up off the ground. The turquoise and silver flashed in the harsh sunlight. He coiled the belt and opened his car door without taking his eyes off Knowles. He tossed the belt casually onto the passenger seat.

"I wasn't going to hang myself over a speeding ticket. That wasn't necessary."

"Who said anything about a speeding ticket? You were driving reckless, boy."

"What, rapping my pipes on the bridge back there?"

"That and them lane changes, crossing lanes repeatedly."

"Officer, there were no other cars front or back as far as I could see. Maybe a block either way."

"Oh, and the law takes a backseat whenever you decide?"

"What's that mean?"

"It means you get to make up the rules as you go along? Multiple lane changes without signaling, unnecessary noise, thirty-five in a thirty? All okay because you say so?"

"I thought you bent the rules on speed. I thought thirty-five was inside the margin of error."

"Whoo-ee, listen to the fancy talk! Margin of error—I like the sound of that. We'll see if it holds water with Judge Montoya."

"There won't be a judge. I'll plead guilty on the back of the ticket, send in the fine, and go on with life. Sorry but wiser."

"Don't work like that, genius. I gotta haul you in while we check the registration."

"I can follow you on my ride."

"No, the bike stays here. I'll send a flatbed because it's gonna be confiscated."

"You can't confiscate my bike for a minor traffic violation. That's against the law. Nor can you take me into custody. I'm allowed to sign for the ticket and go on my way."

"Says who, genius?"

Knowles lifted his chin. "Says me. I'm gonna be a lawyer. I know these things."

"A lawyer! Whoo-ee, we got us a big fish here! Let me tell you something, mister lawyer. I don't give a goddam if you're a priest out of the Vatican. Everyone has to bail out of a felony charge after he goes before a judge. That's how it works around here."

"Did I hear you correctly? You said felony?"

"Hands behind your back!"

Knowles complied, and the cop slipped a pair of silver bracelets around his wrists.

"Felony? Did you say felony?"

"You can read all about it in the court papers. Now take a deep breath and climb in."

The cop swung the rear door open. Knowles slowly climbed in and leaned back against the cuffs. They tore at his wrists. He cringed as the car turned and carved around the Cyclone. It might last an hour until someone grabbed it and carted it off. He turned around and looked out the back window. Abandoning the bike was almost too painful to watch.

They lurched across a busy intersection on a yellow. At a fairly high rate of speed, they maneuvered to the South Loop. At the second stoplight, on the west side of the Loop, the cop made a right and drove slowly down to the end of the street. They pulled up to a squat brick building with antennas sprouting haphazardly from the roof. Several law enforcement vehicles were parked out front. A maple tree spread its branches over the walkway leading to the entrance and the Chicago Police Department sign. They turned in at the last open spot.

The cop waited impatiently while Knowles slid out of the backseat. He jerked him upright, then roughly turned him around and prodded him toward a side entrance marked *Law Enforcement Only.*

First came booking. Knowles posed full-on then sideways for the camera, then the cuffs came off for fingerprinting. "What's his name?" the desk clerk asked the arresting officer.

"Uh, Grant Smith."

Knowles looked up, alarmed. "No, look at my ID. I'm Knowles Gresham."

"No, you're not," said the cop. "You're Grant Smith. Use that name, Harold."

Harold nodded and furiously pounded his typewriter. Once the booking was complete, Knowles was shoved down a long hall to a jail cell. There they waited; evidently, the arresting officer had no keys to the cell.

"You'll be going before Judge Montoya within twenty-four hours," he told Knowles.

"What am I being held for?" Knowles asked. "All misdemeanors in this state are bailable offenses, and I'd like to post bail now. You really can't hold me like this."

The cop, who had been turning away, turned right back. "Come again?"

"I said you can't hold me like this. I have a right to bail out of here."

"Listen to the genius," laughed the cop. "Mr. Lawyer is unhappy."

A jailer appeared behind the arresting officer. He pushed by. Knowles sized him up: a big, burly guy with a gray-haired chest, cop blues, but no necktie. The gun on his hip was almost as long as his arm. He looked Knowles over then produced a ring of keys off his belt. He opened the cell door and stepped inside.

"Disappear," he said over his shoulder to the road cop. The young cop that had arrested Knowles did as he was told. The door at the end of the hall closed behind him.

The jailer reached out and jerked Knowles into the cell with him. "Someone said you're a lawyer, boy."

"I plan to be. And I'd like to post bail and get on my way."

"Well, why don't we take you across the street to the magistrate right now and get that done?"

Knowles moved toward the cell door. "I think that's exactly what the law requires. And thank you for this."

The burly cop checked the silvers around Knowles's wrists. "Too tight?"

"Just a little," Knowles said, "If you could just—"

Without warning, the cop yanked a sap out of his utility belt and swung it at Knowles' head. The sap caught him just forward of the left ear. He cried out and crumpled to his knees. His mind went blank, leaving him unable to form any thought, unable to speak or defend himself. He flexed his arms behind his back. Then he slumped forward, resting on his forehead and knees, off-balance and defenseless, unable to get up. He struggled against the handcuffs behind his back. He fought to raise his head; he tried to speak. The cop swung the sap a second time, catching Knowles flat across the nose. When the cartilage shattered and the nose collapsed, blood went everywhere. Knowles' white T-shirt was sprayed with thick red blood. It ran across the floor. He fell onto his side and instinctively folded his legs. So the cop struck a third time, bashing Knowles' right knee. Bones cracked, and the leg jerked uselessly. This time he didn't move.

"Please," Knowles muttered through the blood and pain and the darkness inside his head. "Please."

"Please? Why don't you run over and file the papers in court, Mr. Lawyer? Maybe that will save your stinking lawyer ass."

"I didn't...do...anything...wrong," Knowles managed to say. "Please. A judge."

"Oh, you'll get to see Judge Montoya soon enough. But you'll wish you hadn't, not after he hears how you attacked me in this cell and I had to defend myself. Judge Montoya hates violence. And he hates lawyers, too, by the way. He used to be one himself, but they pulled his license. Now you lie there and try to sleep it off."

"Please, I—"

This time the sap caught him across the ear. His eyes closed and his body pitched sideways onto the floor, wholly out of control. He wet his pants and blacked out.

When the cop was satisfied his prisoner was unconscious, he stood upright and moved the toe of his boot against the prisoner's hands. He removed the handcuffs. Then he applied the full weight of his massive body to the hands. Bones crunched, but the prisoner made no outcry.

"Now write up some papers," the cop laughed. "Let's see how that works with those hands."

He hurried outside the cell where he paused and, grabbing the badge above his heart, ripped his shirt open as if he had been attacked. There would be photographs, evidence of the assault he'd fought to ward off.

"A good night's sleep provided courtesy of Delmar Crivets, Mr. Lawyer. Nighty-night."

Chapter 3

Knowles regained consciousness in the dark. His hands throbbed, but he couldn't see why. His gaze followed the ceiling to the high windows. He could make out stars hanging in the sky.

Lying on the cold cell floor, he took inventory. The blood in his nose was coagulated; he couldn't breathe except through his mouth. His nose burned and ached, and he thought better of touching it for fear it would bleed again.

He tried pushing up from the floor with his left hand and cried out in pain. The fingers didn't work, and any attempt to brace them on the concrete produced an almost heart-stopping agony. But he managed to draw himself to a sitting position. He tried to stand without using his hands, but the muscles were frozen in his lower back and upper legs. He couldn't move without waves of pain seizing him. He had no doubt: he had been kicked while unconscious. Especially the ribcage, where every breath made him weep.

He gingerly lifted his left hand. Electric pain signals shot back up his arm, but he didn't think bones were broken. The fingers touched the side of his head. The swelling was prominent and flexible, like a raw hamburger patty. He pushed on it and felt the blood and fluids beneath move around. Again, excruciating pain.

Then he realized he was seeing double. There were two windows, but only one of them was real. He knew this because he could make the two into one by closing an eye.

Proceeding south on his body with the inventory, he came to his pants. The denim was soaked. He didn't remember his heroics at the river. He only thought he had wet himself. Then he felt the cold from the cell floor wracking his body with violent shivers. He wrapped his arms across his chest and leaned forward, but he couldn't stop shaking.

So, he just sat there, shivering and wet, hurting beyond anything he'd ever felt. So far beyond, he had nothing to compare it to.

He would have given everything he owned just then for one shotgun and a key to his cell. Chicago would never stop talking about the hurt he would put on this police department, especially the thug who had worked him over.

As his eyes adjusted, he thought he could make out a bunk at his feet. He wondered if he might use the bed frame to pull himself up to his knees.

With all the strength in his mid-section—which was considerable—he rolled and came onto his knees. At the same moment, he reached out for the bunk with his all-but-useless hand. Sure enough, there was a metal frame under the mattress. He laid hold of that and pushed himself into a crouch. He turned sideways to the bed. With his remaining strength quickly draining away, he lowered himself down. The mattress supported him head to toe like a cloud. There was no blanket, but that didn't matter. He was asleep in seconds—probably the worst thing a head injury victim could do, but there was no one to tell him otherwise.

He awoke later, how long he'd been asleep he wasn't sure. Dizziness washed over him, and he puked down the side of his face. Then it all came up until there was only bile that bubbled from his stomach. He swallowed hard. He was dehydrated and thirsty, but there was no sink that he could see. Nothing.

Now sleep came on, and he didn't move again. Not for hours.

Deep into the night, a sudden bright light brought him to the surface of his dreamless sleep. He opened his eyes and found himself staring at a flashlight.

He turned his face away from the glare. Fully expecting to be sapped, he closed his eyes and steeled himself against the pain that was coming. But then someone spoke.

"You sons-of-bitching wops just want to kill police. Am I right, boy?"

Knowles recognized the voice as belonging to the grizzly bear who had worked him over. He lay motionless, holding his breath, doing everything he could to go unnoticed.

Then, without warning, came the sickening slap! Sap against human flesh and bone. But it wasn't his own. Gingerly, he opened his eyes.

"You look the hell the other way, lawyer-boy," cried Grizzly. "This ain't about you!"

Knowles did as he was told, turning his face to the wall along his bunk.

It happened again, the loud slap, followed by the grunts of human suffering that went beyond mere words. Then it slapped down yet again. This time, Knowles heard a body hit the floor with a thud and a whoosh of expelled air. Someone's lungs had just emptied from the force of the fall. He heard a man gasping, fighting to bring oxygen into his empty lungs. Then a soft sobbing took over.

"You fuckin' knock that off, you fuckin' greaseball."

The man replied through his howls, "Alphonse, asshole!"

"Look at you. Crying in my jail? I'm about to give you something to cry about, mister!"

Knowles clenched his eyes tighter and prayed that the man would restrain himself, would stop talking. And his prayer was answered. The man shut up and avoided another sap attack.

"Know what I'm gonna do to you boys if any of this gets out? I'm gonna cut your balls off, that's what. If even one of you lets onto Judge Montoya, I'm gonna de-nut you both. That's right, boys, you've got each other's nuts in your hand!" Grizzly's voice broke into a long peal of laughter as he considered his threat.

Knowles wanted to speak up but knew he couldn't. He would be sapped again and maybe killed. Or permanently brain damaged. Knowing this, he kept his head turned to the wall, half-expecting at any moment a good-night sap from Grizzly.

But it never came. Instead, the cell door closed behind the jailer as he walked out, locked the cell door, then trod down the long hallway. They were alone, Knowles and the new man. In spite of his searing pain, Knowles knew he wanted to help. He knew what it was like to lie on the floor in your piss and wonder if you were dying.

"Hey," Knowles whispered, "can you hear me?"

Long silence, then stirring on the floor below. "Wha—what?"

"I'm Knowles. I got here today, too. He beat me, too. My nose and hand are broken. My teeth are chipped off. What about you?"

"Cannot say for sure."

Knowles rolled onto his side. He swept his good hand down along the floor. Sure enough, there was a leg down there inside a wet pants leg.

"Can you see my hand?"

"No. I felt it on my leg."

"Okay, if it's okay with you, I'm going to put it on your leg again. You grab hold so I can pull you up. That work for you?"

"Yes, sir."

"Okay, here comes my hand."

He swept his throbbing hand down and once again felt the wet leg. This time he left his hand in place until fingers closed around his wrist. It was just high enough on his arm that his fingers were spared. Surprisingly, for what the new guy had just endured, his was a firm grip.

"Okay, I'm gonna pull you up."

Knowles rolled onto his back, pulling the man with him.

"Ohhhh!"

"I know. Everything hurts. Can you see yet?"

"One eye can see. I have no idea what I'm looking at."

"Let's get you up on your knees. I'll try to get you up on this bunk with me."

Long silence.

Then, "I don't know. Who are you?"

"Knowles Gresham. I'm a guy who got dragged off his motorcycle and beat up when they brought me here. I'm not gonna hurt you. I'm not gonna make a play. Okay?"

"Okay. Hold on now."

The man pulled mightily against Knowles's wrist, and Knowles almost lost him. But he managed to hang on. Then the man was upon his knees, his back level with the bed.

"Okay, try to stand as best you can, then roll down on this bed. I'll move over to the wall, so there's room."

The man relaxed his grip, and Knowles moved up against the wall. The stone facing was cold against his back, and he shivered. Then he lost control, and muscle contractions wracked his arms and legs as the cold did its work.

Suddenly, a man was beside him on the thin mattress. He, too, was shivering and shaking.

"There's no blanket," Knowles said, "but tell you what. Can you get on your side?"

"Facing or away?"

"Facing away. I'm gonna spoon you. Give you my body heat."

"You sure you ain't—"

"Look, man, you don't wanna go into shock. Now, do as I say."

He felt the thin mattress bunch up and knew the man had rolled over. Knowles took a deep breath and closed the distance between them. Now he had the man spooned and could lay his arm across him. The man's back was wet, and the cold instantly transferred into Knowles's chest and legs, but he didn't move away, staying entangled with the newcomer to prevent shock.

A short while later they were both asleep. Knowles was awakened once by someone sobbing without noise, but he realized it was only his bedmate. He closed his eyes and went back to sleep.

Chapter 4

At dawn, Grizzly returned. "You boys follow me. You gonna take showers."

Grizzly came into the cell then stopped abruptly. "You gotta be shitting me! You boys paired up already? Anybody gettin' any?"

He was referring to the two of them clinging together on the bed, where they had fought off the freezing night air in their wet clothes. They might have died from exposure without the other's body heat. They pulled apart the moment the jailer came in, but it was too late. He had seen them together.

Knowles watched as his bedmate inched off the bed and tried to stand. He was shaky, but he maintained a stooped standing posture. Knowles followed, which immediately set off a coughing jag that all but ripped his ribs out of his body. The pain was searing and felt like he was being kicked all over again. "Okay," he said, coming up almost vertical. "Where's the shower?"

"Bad news, girls. We're out of hot water this morning. You go first into the hall," he said, pointing to Knowles. "Down to the other end and then through the door when it buzzes. That's the showers."

Knowles led the way to the end of the hall. Buzzed through the door, the two prisoners found themselves in a concrete-floored shower area with dirty tile walls. The place smelled like urine. There were two shower heads, one on each side of the small room.

"Let's shake a leg," cried Grizzly. "Shuck them clothes and wash up."

Removing their damp clothes, the men made a point of not looking at each other. They left their clothes in two separate piles and stepped under the showers. There was only one faucet for each shower-head. Knowles knew it was coming—no hot, just cold. He twisted the knob and waited while the shower head chugged and sprang to life. Sucking in a deep breath, he ducked inside the spray.

Instant shock, the water was so cold. Knowles gasped and forced himself to soap up while Grizzly watched. The man was smiling as he observed his prisoners shaking, cringing under the icy water.

"Turn on the hot water, boys!" cried Grizzly. Then, "Oh, that's right, there ain't any!"

The jailer's laughter filled the small room and echoed off the tile walls. Knowles closed his eyes and rinsed off before spinning the faucet until the water stopped. He was shaking uncontrollably and flapping his arms.

"Now get those clothes on," Grizzly ordered.

"What about dry clothes?" Knowles asked.

"I didn't see no suitcases. You boys smuggle in dry clothes?"

"What about a towel?" asked Alphonse.

"Towel? You shittin' me? You think this is a hotel, boy? Now get them goddam clothes on before I start swinging!"

Dripping wet, the cellmates struggled back into their clothes without speaking. They were miserable, but they knew it wouldn't solve anything to complain. It was what it was.

"What time's breakfast?" Knowles asked Grizzly when he was dressed.

Grizzly smiled evilly. "That's the time! You got me hatin' on you, boy!"

"Just asking," Knowles answered.

A half hour later, they were herded across the street. It was a combined courthouse/city hall affair, reasonably new since the original building had been burned to the ground ten years earlier.

Knowles, ordered to lead the way, turned where instructed once they were inside the building. Then they entered a small courtroom, complete with an American flag and a state flag. The room was dark and cold and looked as forlorn as Knowles felt.

Without warning and fanfare, Judge Rafael Montoya, a dark man wearing khaki slacks, a white western shirt, and a bolo tie, entered and climbed two steps to the judge's chair. He spoke to no one as he arranged the items on the desk before him. Then he looked up.

"Officer Crivets, who are these fine gentlemen?" So Grizzly was Crivets.

"Judge, the greaseball is Alphonse Capone. The kid is Grant Smith."

"Correction," said Knowles, "my correct name is Knowles Gresham."

"Yes, judge." Crivets smiled. "This one had no ID, so we identified him through his motorcycle registration. Grant Smith is his name. Or the bike's stolen and this is someone else."

"It's my motorcycle," Knowles protested.

"Then that makes you Grant Smith," Crivets smirked. "Now shut up and let the judge talk."

"Thank you, Officer Crivets. So, Mr. Capone and Mr. Smith, let's see what we're going to do with you. Mr. Capone, it appears you tried to outrun the arresting officer in your Buick. That's what the ticket in front of me says. Fleeing to avoid arrest is a felony in this state, sir. Very serious. And Mr. Smith—"

"Gresham—"

"Mr. Smith, you're charged with grand theft for the theft of the motorcycle."

"It's my bike, Judge."

"Then your name must be Grant Smith. That's who the ticket says is the registered owner. But you're saying your name is Gresham, so the bike is stolen. The court is charging you with grand theft in addition to the arresting officer's charges on these tickets, which include reckless driving, speeding, and possession of a controlled substance, cannabis."

"Judge, I don't use—"

"Careful, Mr. Smith, anything you say before me is being taken down and can be used against you in a trial. For that reason, you're admonished to remain silent. These are both felonies—serious felonies. But they are bailable offenses. So the court sets bail on each case at one-thousand dollars. Cash bonds only will be accepted."

"Judge—" Knowles began.

"Careful, Mr. Smith. Court reporter, remember?"

"Judge, my uncle is an alderman. His name is Leon Gresham. I've never heard of a single count of grand theft or fleeing to avoid that required a thousand-dollar bail. The ordinary bail is one-hundred dollars for either charge. Neither of us has a thousand-dollars cash to bail out. That's obvious."

"Mr. Capone? Do you have one-thousand dollars to post?"

"Not with me," said the smaller man. "I wouldn't give it to you anyhow."

"Then you're remanded to the custody of the sheriff. Now, Mr. Crivets, will these men be working with the sheriff's posse?"

"Yes, Your Honor," said Crivets.

"My Uncle Leon is gonna be furious about this," Knowles said.

"Hold it!" snapped the judge. "Did you say your uncle is Leon Gresham?"

"Yes, sir."

"Alderman Leon Gresham?"

"Yes, sir."

"Mr. Crivets, take these boys across the street and turn them loose. All charges are hereby dismissed."

Knowles felt his heart rise in his chest. Beside him, Alphonse Capone was grinning. He poked Knowles in the side. "I owe you big, buddy," said his cellmate. "I won't forget."

They were hustled back across the street, where Crivets suddenly pushed them away and turned and disappeared back inside the police building. Knowles followed him inside and requested his motorcycle key from the attendant. The key was turned over without a word; Knowles went back outside. Capone was long gone.

The Cyclone was parked in the street in a police slot. Knowles kicked the starter, and the V-Twin caught and purred.

Riding away on River Street, he never looked back. And he had no idea which direction Capone had gone.

Their time together had passed.

Chapter 5

Knowles C. Gresham was born in England in 1898. Six years later, he was transplanted to Chicago for safekeeping and raising by his Uncle Leon. The reason for the move was his father's incurable tuberculosis. Father and uncle agreed the move was in Knowles's best interest.

In 1910, Chicago was well on the way to becoming the noise capital of the world. There was cobblestone around the Dearborn Street Station, making the Model T's and Buick's rumble and clatter as they delivered and retrieved passengers from the station. Horse-drawn carts, the customary transportation for the ragmen, produce men, and junk collectors of the day, clogged the streets. Horses' eye blinkers kept equine heads low and enticements out of view as the owners went about their business.

Dearborn Street Station, adjacent to Printers' Row, was the oldest of the six intercity train stations serving downtown. A majestic clock tower, rising high into the smoky, dirty air of a giant city readying itself for the industrial boom, looked down on trains called the *Super Chief* and the *El Capitan*, carrying celebrities to and from Hollywood. The Station was the centerpiece of the South Loop area of Chicago during its teens.

While the city was growing and mushrooming at its seams, the Chicago political machine was already in full swing. The political scene let organized crime flourish to the point that Chicago cops often earned more money in plain brown bags than from the city.

A rich opulence characterized 1910 fashion in America in contrast with the somber practicality of garments worn during World War 1. Men's trousers were creased and cuffed at the ankles. With the coming Jazz Age, skirts rose from floor length to well above the ankle. Women began to bob their hair, everybody who was anybody was keeping up with the exciting new fashions associated with the Jazz Age of the 1920s.

Leon Gresham, Knowles' uncle, was a transplant from Southern England. He determined he would become as American as anyone else. One way was keeping up with styles in clothing. He wore his tailored suits and vests in vibrant colors and cuts. He preferred pinstripes, heavily starched white shirts with detachable collars, necktie pins that looked like expensive diamonds, and two-tone shoes—all of it topped off with a derby hat for the sidewalks and roadways.

Uncle Leon was an alderman and entrepreneur offering day-old vegetables and day-old baked goods from his neighborhood grocery on Polk Street. From a young age, Knowles swept his Uncle Leon's store, wrangled the garbage at the end of the day, and at night would accompany Uncle Leon to aldermanic meetings where the city's business was transacted. Most often, the sessions involved the three construction czars who had commandeered the city's road-building business and were making a killing turning third-class dirt and cobblestone roads into brand-spanking-new asphalt ribbons of highway across Chicago.

One of these czars was Roscoe H. Naply, an Irishman who ran his business with clubs and guns aimed at anyone who tried to interfere with his builds. Roscoe left behind a desperate and starving Ireland and came over the Atlantic ready to fight with anyone who got in the way of his success in America.

By the age of twenty-one, Knowles, now grown into a strapping young man, was driving a dump truck for Roscoe H. Naply. Road construction had all but brought the city to a standstill. "Throw a rock in any direction," the saying went, "and you'll hit a road paving machine."

On Good Friday, in 1920, Knowles witnessed Naply's encounter with a particular policeman from the Chicago PD. The cop's name was Wilhelm, and evidently, he was a good one because he refused to allow Roscoe's earth-moving equipment and paving machines to block both sides of a roadway, unlike the police officers who'd been bought and who looked the other way, citizen traffic be damned. If the entire city had to go an extra mile to avoid a Naply excavation, so be it.

Wilhelm, however, an honest patrolman, wasn't buying it. On that early spring day, he parked his squad car in the center of Adams Street and refused to allow Naply's men to block the road in both directions. Furious upon hearing the news, Roscoe Naply left the seclusion of his trailer and strode defiantly up to the cop who was standing in the middle of the torn-up road. Naply stopped inches away from the cop and sucker-punched him before a word was said. Knowles Gresham witnessed the beating that ensued. Waiting in a line of dump trucks to lay down his load of dirt, Knowles saw that Naply wasn't letting up even when he had the cop on the ground. Fists rained down on the hapless law officer and boots connected violently with his ribs and head. Within a minute, the cop was lying face-down in the mud, making no move to resist. Even from fifty feet away, Knowles could see the cop was unconscious. Naply, however, persisted in beating and kicking, and throwing off his employees who laid hands on their boss in a vain attempt to pull him away and let the man live.

Knowles couldn't sit by while one man killed another, no matter the basis of the dispute. He had watched the whole thing and thought the dispute was minor and warranted no attack, given that the cop's only trespass was to enforce a law requiring one-half of a street to remain open to vehicle passage at all times.

Knowles stubbed his Lucky Strike into the truck's ashtray, threw open the door, and climbed down out of his rig. Without looking right or left he broke into a trot and came up behind his employer, who was leveling his boots at the unconscious law officer's face, leaving it a bloody mess. Knowles was big and strong like all young men who'd known only hard physical labor their entire working life. Naply was large and round, but his physical conditioning and strength were just half that of Knowles's.

When he felt Knowles pulling him off of the cop, he went into a rage and pulled his .38 caliber handgun from an inside coat pocket. He broke free and turned on Knowles, pointing the gun directly at the truck driver's chest. Knowles advanced on the man nevertheless. Just as he was about to club the owner with a huge, mighty fist, Naply pulled the trigger. The bullet ripped into Knowles's right chest, piercing his lung, and knocked him a step backward. But it didn't stop him. On he came, laying hands on the gun before Naply could fire it again. He whipped the gun away from his employer and clubbed the man down to his knees and then into the mud before slumping forward himself and losing consciousness. Now three men lay in the mud, unconscious and bleeding, as others on the job site called for ambulances and police.

The official vehicles arrived, and the men were transported to three different hospitals.

The cop regained consciousness after four days in a coma and seven surgeries, three of which rebuilt his face where orbital sockets had been crushed, his nose displaced to one side, and top and bottom front teeth dislodged and lost. Chief White of the Chicago PD personally visited the injured officer. Pictures were taken of the Chief with the patrolman and distributed by Chicago's three newspapers, evidence of the Chief's one-on-one support of his officers.

Investigating officers were interrogated. Quite quickly, the Chief became aware of the heroic intervention of Knowles Gresham, who by now had been treated and released from the hospital with a wound that was healing without any sequelae. He was going to be okay. But, said the evening news, he had of course been fired from his job. Chicago, being a mob-owned town in 1919, would refuse to hire young Knowles on any job site or in any other capacity. He might as well move to another state, said those in the know.

Which caught the attention of Chief White. He wasted no time. On the Monday after Easter Sunday, he invited Knowles to visit him at City Hall and used the occasion for a photo op. Pictures of the Chief with the brave truck driver were splashed across front pages. Knowles was now credited with saving the life of a police officer even though it cost him his job and would, essentially, turn him out on the streets to scrounge for food and shelter.

Following the photography session, the Chief invited Knowles to speak with him in the Chief's private office. He was blunt and wasted no words. Would Knowles like to apply to the city police force for work? Absolutely, said Knowles without hesitation. After which, the Chief buzzed an aide into the office, applications and health forms were filled out while the Chief looked on, and the application was approved. Young Knowles was welcomed to the police force as a new officer before lunch on that cold Monday in April.

Chapter 6

Knowles C. Gresham was six-four, 235 pounds, with a clear complexion and bright gray eyes that were sometimes blue. He was a man who'd had no problem getting time with the neighborhood ladies at movies and dinners. He passed through the police academy with ease, graduating first in his class. He was officially awarded his badge and sidearm on July 15, and he'd never been happier. Working for an all-Irish police department didn't happen for Englishmen like Knowles Gresham, but there you were.

In 1920, Knowles married the beautiful Natalia Young, a distant relative of Brigham Young, who had moved with his people to Utah. Natalia's father was a cousin to the religious leader, but he had always refused anything to do with the new religion, instead choosing to manage his fleet of river barges hauling grain up and down the Illinois and Mississippi Rivers. The money poured into Hank Young's bank account like the soybeans his boats unloaded into the hundred-foot granaries dotting the rivers. He became wealthy, then wealthier, and finally ridiculously wealthy.

His daughter, Natalia, raised in decency and common sense, graduated the University of Chicago and took a job as a welfare worker, which is how she met Knowles Gresham. The two began going out for dinners and enjoying a modest nightlife. After a year, they married on the grounds of Natalia's childhood home in Evanston, which featured Knowles in his police dress blues surrounded by fifty other police officers clad likewise who danced and chatted and enjoyed the after-party in a style they had rarely known before.

Knowles and Natalia had a kitchen-table conference two weeks post-wedding.

"You know I earn but a piddling compared to the men in your family," Knowles said to his wife over coffee and cream cookies.

Natalia laughed. "I didn't marry for your money."

"Oh no? You could have fooled me!" Knowles joked. "Here, all along, I thought you were after my assets."

"Of which there are none," his new wife said. "Which is just how I like it. We're going to raise our kids in an environment of honor and trust instead of money and belongings. We both know this is a healthier choice and will make it more likely our offspring will grow up to be happy and respected adults."

Natalia was light-years ahead of her time. But it was the sociologist inside of her. UC had trained her to think like a do-gooder for the less fortunate, and UC's lessons had been firmly implanted in Natalia's mind and character. She was, when it was all said and done, a woman of the people, while her husband was likewise a man of the people. And so they set off to embrace life, always bent on doing the right thing no matter the personal cost.

* * *

Tragedy struck the Gresham household a scant five years after the marriage ceremony. Natalia Gresham was stricken with polio and confined to an iron lung, unable to exist outside of her metal cocoon. Bravely determined and prayerful, the Greshams went ahead with life, determined to see it out, ever-hopeful that a cure for Natalia was just around the corner and that she would soon be fully restored to health.

But the cure didn't arrive. Instead, the Greshams were forced to hire around-the-clock nursing care for Natalia so that Knowles could continue working at the Chicago Police Department, supporting his stricken wife.

Nurses came and went. The staff was always turning over, with one exception. The midnight shift consisted of a young Filipino nurse by the name of Martha Bautista, and Martha let it be known that she considered Natalia to be her mission in life. A devout Catholic, Martha had lived for a year in a Manila convent and had seriously contemplated life as a nun. But her scientific mind and desire to see America moved her along to nursing school with a specialty in epidemiology. After arriving in the U.S., Martha became well-known in the Chicago medical community as a nurse who knew as much about polio as most physicians. Maybe even more.

Martha met Natalia, and they clicked. Natalia stood for everything Martha held sacred— church, home, family, community welfare, a dedication to helping the less fortunate—Natalia had lived it all. Martha was offered a permanent job caring for Natalia. She accepted without hesitation. Martha's restlessness came to a full stop. In Natalia, she had found her life's work. She was home.

She was home in another sense, as well. A spare bedroom was offered to Martha. Knowles and Natalia encouraged the young nurse to take them up on the offer; she would have her privacy, and she would have easy access to her work, just down the hall in what once had been the dining room, now where the iron lung and Natalia were ensconced. Martha slowly warmed to the idea and finally accepted. Touched as she was by the Gresham's need for her presence, Martha surrendered any resistance she'd harbored to moving in. Twenty-four hours later, the bedroom was all hers, full of boxes and two suitcases and a hundred pounds of medical books that required Knowles to build a cinder block and pine wood bookcase to contain them all.

Martha was soon part of the family. She went above and beyond her role as the nighttime nurse. She took to grocery shopping for the family, preparing all meals, and watching over Natalia. She was extra attentive during the stricken woman's afternoon crying sessions when her predicament overwhelmed her. Natalia was brought to tears on almost a daily basis while her husband was away at the police station.

The crying sessions were kept secret from Knowles. Natalia had Martha's pledge that the truth of what went on would never be made known to her husband.

Martha wasn't proud, keeping secrets from her employer, but she went along. She was a woman of principle, still, and she found herself increasingly uncomfortable keeping her patient's emotional health a secret from Knowles. But she forced herself anyway, despite the fact she worshipped the man and wanted more than anything to let him in on the real truth.

But she didn't. She learned she could keep a secret.

Which was one day going to mean everything.

Knowles was now a popular member of the long blue line, a blue line increasingly confronted by the Chicago Mob. He was known to be a "can-do" officer and his superiors had a habit of going to him for the difficult problems. One difficult problem was building to a climax as there was a madman on the loose in Chicago.

Alphonse Capone was waiting.

Chapter 7

Born of an immigrant family in Brooklyn in 1899, Al Capone quit school after the sixth grade and became associated with a notorious street gang. Johnny Torrio was the leader, and among the other members was Lucky Luciano, who would later attain his own notoriety.

Johnny Torrio, now calling his empire the Outfit, competed with other gangsters in Chicago for the bootlegging business. Despite this, Torrio was able to reach a truce with Dean O'Banion, the leader of the Irish North Side Gang. The Chicago Outfit operated in South Chicago while Dean O'Banion worked out of the North Side. Torrio also had allied with the Sicilian Genna crime family that worked out of Little Italy in the city's center.

The truce with the North Side fell apart after Torrio's protégé, Al Capone, took over the empire in 1925 when Torrio, severely wounded in an assassination attempt, surrendered control and retired to Brooklyn. Capone had built a fearsome reputation within the vicious gang rivalries of the period as he acquired and retained "racketeering rights" to several areas of Chicago. That reputation grew as rival gangs were eliminated or nullified, and the suburb of Cicero became, in effect, a fiefdom of the Capone mob.

During Prohibition, Al Capone saw an opportunity for himself and the Outfit in Chicago to make money and to expand their criminal empire by racketeering small businesses further. With Capone taking the role of a businessman and partner to small business owners, the Outfit had a legitimate way to source their money, which avoided unnecessary attention from law enforcement.

This culminated in the St. Valentine's Day Massacre in 1929. The St. Valentine's Day Massacre on February 14, might be regarded as the culminating violence of the Chicago gang era. Seven members of the "Bugs" Moran mob were machine-gunned against a garage wall by rivals posing as police. The massacre was pinned on the Capone mob, although Al himself was in Florida.

By now, Knowles Gresham had made his way through the ranks until finally being promoted to sergeant around the same time Capone came into his own and gunned down his enemies on St. Valentine's Day. Knowles was on the scene of the murder five minutes after it happened. He spent the rest of that day and part of the night directing uniformed personnel in securing the scene and aiding in the preservation of evidence.

Capone's picture captured top-of-the-fold position on all Chicago newspapers as Suspect Number One. However, Capone had been beaten so severely on the night he spent in jail with Knowles that Knowles didn't recognize him.

Three days into the investigation, Knowles was inflamed with hatred of Capone for the indiscriminate murder of his enemies, evidently without fear of the police. Knowles, driving home that night, swore an oath to see Capone dead in the ground inside one year.

* * *

After the St. Valentine's day slaughter, Knowles was assigned full-time to the FBI-Chicago PD Joint Task Force, created to end the notorious gangster's career. "Death or bars," the agents said in greeting, meaning their goal for Capone was to shoot him dead or send him to prison for life. Death or bars.

The mass shooting had the effect of sealing Capone's fate for the Joint Task Force. A final line had been crossed.

However, despite its motivation, the Joint Task Force remained stymied. For Capone had assumed the model taken on by all gangsters, dictators, and criminal syndicates: the head of the organization never got within one man of any crime. If there was to be a murder, while Capone might've ordered it, it was carried out by men several times removed. Capone was untouchable.

Street crimes then—the violent type that could send Capone to the electric chair—were never going to be traceable back to Capone. Meetings were held by the Joint Task Force, meetings open to any and all ideas how the team might be able to bring Capone down. One night, Martha and Knowles had a conversation just before lights out in the Gresham household.

"He gets money from crime, correct?" the nurse asked Knowles.

"Yes, lots and lots of it."

"It's simple then. Does Mr. Capone report his income on his tax return?"

It was a jarring question. No one had bothered to ask it before.

Knowles jumped up from the couch and dropped to one knee in front of Martha. "You just put the most notorious gangster in history in prison. Thank you."

Knowles quickly took Martha's simple idea before the Task Force. He told his colleagues that a particular nurse had had the brilliant idea of putting together a financial crimes case against

Capone. The idea instantly struck a chord with the FBI. While attribution of the genius idea in the news media probably would've gotten Martha murdered, in-house the gambit became known as "Martha's X-Ray," in consideration for the thorough review about to be undertaken of Capone's financial life.

The most obvious first inquiry was Capone's federal income tax returns. Accountants and CPA's were called in by the feds. At times, more IRS agents were occupying the local FBI's visitors' offices than visiting FBI agents. They were everywhere inside the building, analyzing and working up what was known as an attribution case against Capone.

The attribution case was simple. Capone's mansion in Cicero meant he was earning at least $150,000 per year to afford and maintain a place like that. Attribute $150K income to Capone. Yet his tax returns fell far, far short of that number. But it didn't stop there. Automobiles, clothing, the exorbitant cost of dining and partying the nights away at Chicago's most expensive clubs and restaurants indicated at least another $25,000 a year. And on and on it went, illegal income attributed to Capone based on the cost of Capone's assets and lifestyle.

Capone was grossly under-reporting his income. The FBI and IRS agents were deliriously happy. Knowles became the in-house hero for the whole approach.

Capone was indicted. The lawyers negotiated and argued and fought and negotiated some more. At long last, a settlement was reached.

On June 16, 1931, Al Capone pled guilty to tax evasion and Prohibition charges. He then boasted to the press that he had struck a deal for a two-and-a-half-year sentence, but the presiding judge informed him he, the judge, was not bound by any agreement. Capone then changed his plea to not guilty. Eventually, the case against Capone went to trial in Chicago.

On October 18, 1931, Capone was convicted after trial and on November 24, was sentenced to eleven years in federal prison, fined $50,000 and charged $7,692 for court costs, in addition to $215,000 plus interest due on back taxes.

Champagne flowed the night of November 24 in the offices of the FBI. Knowles was roundly and repeatedly toasted with hoisted champagne flutes. But each time, he raised a hand and reminded the members of the Joint Task Force that it was a woman named Martha who was the genius. "To Martha, then!" cried the agents and officers.

It was just the beginning for Sergeant Gresham, whose role in the top-secret prosecution had caught the eye of the Chicago political machine.

Chapter 8

Franklin D. Roosevelt's crushing defeat of Herbert Hoover in the presidential race of 1932 was perfect timing for all Democrats running for office. While it wouldn't have been said that Knowles Gresham won his Senate seat by riding the coattails of Roosevelt, the hyperactive voting that November all across Chicago certainly inured to Knowles' benefit, and he won his ticket to the U.S. Senate that bleak November day.

It was a snowy day, early winter hung in the air like ghostly sheets of cold and gray. Knowles finally was driven home from his campaign headquarters at seven o'clock the morning after election day, following an all-night vigil at the chalkboard where votes were tallied citywide as they became known.

"Good night, Senator Gresham," the campaign staff bid him as Knowles was leaving the office and its red-white-and-blue political bunting and balloons. He could only smile and wave. He'd come a long way from the boy who'd stepped up and stopped his boss from beating a police officer to death. A very long way.

Upon arriving home that dawn, Knowles went into the dining room and kissed Natalia as she lay inside her iron lung, breathing twenty times per minute on cue.

"We did it," he said to the wife he treasured.

She peered into the overhead mirror that others spoke into when conversing with her. "I'm beyond proud of you, my darling. Congratulations."

He touched her face and brushed her lips with his own. Then he went into the kitchen and poured a cup of coffee from the percolator that Martha kept on simmer day and night.

He returned to Natalia's side, taking his seat in the easy chair he'd placed at her head to stay nearby during his time at home. He balanced his cup and saucer on one knee. He stared at the side of his wife's face, the only noise in the room the "whoosh" of the iron lung as it forced the breath of life into the patient's paralyzed lungs.

Finally, Natalia broke the silence. "You'll be going to Washington without me."

His head jerked upright. "Not at all! You'll go there with me. It's all said and done. Procedures for transporting you and your appliance to Washington are already being looked into by my staff. I wouldn't leave you behind for all the votes in the world, darling Natalia."

Tears rolled down her cheeks. "I was afraid," she whispered.

He set his coffee aside and dropped to his knees beside her. He placed the side of his face against hers. "Never. I'll never leave you, my precious."

"Oh—oh! I'm the luckiest woman on earth. I get to have my Knowles."

Tears streamed from the new senator's eyes. Despite the hell of Natalia's situation, the couple was otherwise blissfully happy with each other. Adoration was more than a word in the Gresham household.

"We'll be together no matter where I go," he promised her. "Never doubt, my love."

"Well, then, how about some music to celebrate? Fire up the Victrola and let's listen to Benny Goodman. We need some Benny!"

"Sure enough."

Minutes later, the sounds of the renowned bandleader filtered through the dining room. Natalia hummed along with the music while Knowles returned to his perch in the easy chair and watched over her.

* * *

They booked their move on the *Capitol Limited*, the train running between Chicago and Washington. The train moved Natalia and Knowles—and Martha—from Chicago to K Street in Washington, D.C. The trip between Union Station and D.C. was slow, arduous, and it was expensive due to the accommodations required for Natalia. But in the end, help wasn't very far away, as the new senator would find was always the case. The railroad made a gift of the cost of the ride to the new senator, but only after the corporate officer in charge had made it known in a letter written to Knowles, requested by Knowles, that the gift was a measure of the railroad's patriotism and nothing more. No beneficence was expected by the railroad in return.

* * *

"I want us to have a son," Natalia one day told her husband.

Knowles stopped in his tracks. Had he just heard his wife correctly? He took his seat beside her. "I don't follow you," he said gently. "Did you say you're sorry we never had a son?"

"No, I said I *want* us to have a son."

"Isn't that impossible now?"

She smiled into the mirror. "Impossible for me, maybe. Not at all impossible for you."

He raised his hands in exasperation before letting them fall back into his lap. "Then I'm baffled, Natalia. I'm not getting this at all."

"Martha loves you."

"Yes, she loves us both. And we love her."

Natalia shook her head. "No, she's actually in love with you. I've spoken to her about it. She finally confessed. I think it's a blessing."

"The University of Chicago did, indeed, turn out a fine liberal when it graduated you, Nat. A little off-kilter, yes, but a liberal's liberal nonetheless. However, Martha is certainly not in love with me. That's all I want to hear about that."

"No, you don't get to boss this one. You're going to be a sperm donor. Martha has agreed to carry our child for me."

"What—?" the senator was struck speechless.

"Yes. She loves us; she's committed her life to us. She's ready to carry our child. There needn't be any lust on your part, Knowles. Just a donor."

The senator was again at a loss for words. His ears were burning, and his heart raced wildly in his chest. Deep down, his biggest regret was Natalia's failed health, of course. But lying there in his heart, kept silent by his willpower, was the wish that they'd had children. Especially a son to carry on the Gresham name. Now his precious Natalia was presenting him with the possibility of seeing this dream to fruition. A coupling with Martha? In all honesty, that possibility had never once crossed his mind, committed as he was to his wife. She was his all; nothing else mattered.

But he also knew she, too, regretted never having a child. She, too, was crushed she'd missed out on that blessing. So she'd broached the issue with Martha. She'd seen how Martha looked at Knowles—with total respect, yes, but also with a light in her eyes, a lilt in her voice, that wasn't there those times when Knowles was absent from the home. Not there at all. Natalia found her second-best-friend in the world transparent—in a good sense. Her love for Natalia's husband was obvious, repressed, and all but tragic since it would never be fulfilled. But not terrible to Natalia; she would settle for nothing less than a fresh new start, this time with a new Gresham baby in the world.

"Promise me that you'll do this for us, Knowles," Natalia requested.

"I've only just now heard anything about it. I don't know how I feel."

"It doesn't matter how you feel. We need a son, and Martha's willing to lend us her womb. Now you get in there and seduce her and make us a baby. This isn't negotiable."

"My God, you're deadly serious about this."

"I am, Senator. And as far as anyone outside our four walls will ever know, the child is ours—yours and mine."

"How does that work?"

"We change his age. We hold out that he was born before I was struck down with polio. No one will know the difference."

"My constituents will know."

"Not if you don't tell them. The boy is yours and mine. We've kept him out of the public eye because we didn't want another Lindbergh baby."

In 1932, Charles Augustus Lindbergh Jr., 20-month-old son of aviator Charles Lindbergh and Anne Morrow Lindbergh, was abducted from his home in Highfields, New Jersey. Shortly after, his body was discovered nearby. After that, America changed for the worse. Children were no longer safe from harm anywhere in the country. The new reality was the Lindbergh Baby reality.

"We were going to tell the world about our son but decided otherwise when Lucky Lindy's baby was murdered. "

"Yes," said Knowles, "that would make sense, given that during that time I was working with the Joint Task Force and the less anyone knew about our families, the safer we felt. We made a point of keeping our personal lives separate from our daily lives. Privacy was sacrosanct."

"See?" said Natalia. "I rest my case. I am the birth mother of our baby boy. We're going to name him Roland Knowles Gresham."

"Oh, you sound pretty sure of all this."

"I am certain of it."

"Then who am I to argue? You know I'd do anything for you, Nat."

"Now, go. Leave me alone and seduce someone while you're away. Please, Knowles."

He drew a deep breath and leaned back in his chair. He clasped a knee between his hands. So be it, he thought. If that's what my wife wants, who am I to deny her? I'd do anything for her, even and including this.

As Knowles rinsed his coffee cup in the kitchen sink, a single thought repeated in his mind. Martha, the mother of Roland. Really?

* * *

It turned out there was no seduction. Because the seduction of Martha was unnecessary. On a steamy July 4 in 1932, as skyrockets launched from Navy Pier left sparkling arcs of color in the night sky, Martha crept into Knowles' bedroom. She wore a transparent negligee that caught the intermittent light streaming through Knowles's bedside window. At that moment, her full, willing body was revealed beneath, causing Knowles to suck in his breath and find himself the woman's slave. He performed exactly as Martha—ever the nurse—directed him. There was no kissing or other expression of love, just the determined performance of two mammals procreating.

When it was finished, Martha wordlessly pushed up from Knowles's bed and hurried from the room, down the hall to her room, where she went inside and closed the door. She prayed that night for pregnancy; so did Knowles. And so did Natalia, whose hearing was anything but impaired.

Thirty minutes later, Martha, now wearing a robe closed from neck to knee, knocked on Knowles's door before entering. "Let's go see Natalia."

"Right," he said, coming out of a shallow slumber, "see Natalia."

Together they entered Natalia's dining room-medical suite and found the patient wide awake and smiling.

"So," said Natalia in a strong voice, "were we successful tonight?"

Martha and Knowles looked at each other then turned their full attention to Natalia. The trio erupted into peals of laughter as they mentioned the unmentionable over and over.

"He said your name when he was finishing," Martha told Natalia. "Rather, he sharply cried out your name."

Tears appeared in Natalia's eyes. "My Knowles," she spoke into her mirror. Then, "Tell me everything. No secrets among this baby's three parents."

"I don't think so," Knowles replied. "Some things are better left unsaid, Nat."

"Nonsense. If I can't be there in body, then I must be there in spirit. Tell me now, every last caress and thrust. I must know."

Knowing he was defeated, Knowles gamely launched into the coupling. "Well, I was—I was lying on my back. I mean I was—"

"Hush, Knowles," Martha interrupted. "That's not what she wants to hear. She wants to hear the tenderness, the romance."

"But there wasn't any of that," Knowles said.

Martha smiled. "Maybe not for you, the man. But a woman experiences things differently. Why don't you go make us some coffee while I take Natalia through our process?"

"Our process?"

"Oh, yes, our established process," Martha said. "Just in case we need to repeat, we've established a process. Run off, now, while I describe that process for your wife."

"Yes, Knowles," said Natalia. "Martha will have what I need. I'll take my coffee with extra cream this time. It'll help me sleep when we're done here."

Knowles could only shrug and shake his head. He had been excused from the play-by-play. Which suited him just fine. All of which meant Natalia was right: he didn't have the words she needed to hear. So, he left the room, heading for the kitchen and the percolator on the stove.

Chapter 9

Happily seated in Congress in 1933, Knowles was satisfied in his professional life but disappointed with himself in his personal life.

"I'm disappointed," he whispered in the kitchen pantry to Martha one night. She had been searching for a jar of fig jam to go with bread and butter at dinnertime. Knowles came up behind her and said, "I'm disappointed with myself because I can't stop thinking about you." He immediately hated himself for his weakness.

Without turning around, Martha said, "Stop thinking, then. You're a married man, and you love your wife and your wife loves you.

"Well, how do you feel about me, Martha? I know there's something there."

Just two months earlier, Martha had given birth to Roland, Knowles' first son.

"How do I feel? I feel like a broodmare who has just foaled, that's how I feel. Do you mean do I feel something for you, Knowles? Of course, I do. Most women would. But I'd never let my personal feelings come between your Natalia and me."

"But what of us, you and I? Have you considered continuing with me at night? Perhaps sleeping in my room?" He all but choked on his words. He thought himself profoundly wicked but out of control with lust.

"No, I haven't thought of that. Nor would I. Natalia would soon know."

"I don't plan on telling her."

"She'd know. Wives know that kind of thing. Besides which, all she has to do with her mind while she's trapped inside that terrible machine is listen to the noises the house makes. Maybe the occasional Model A passing by outside. She'd hear our lovemaking and die of sadness. I can't do that to her. If it means I don't ever have a man, so be it. Natalia won't be sacrificed for my own selfish needs."

"Well, everything you say makes perfect sense. And is admirable. But I still miss you and want you. Maybe I'm even a little bit in love."

She wheeled on him then, in the pantry, and shoved a jar of fig jam hard against his chest. Her eyes narrowed.

"Never say that to me again, Knowles. If you do, I'll be gone that same hour, and you'll never see me again. Do you understand?"

"I'm sorry. I've just really jumped the rails, haven't I?"

"Indeed."

"Yes, I have."

"Go wash up for dinner. Tell Natalia food's on the way."

"Okay."

"Now, scoot!"

He didn't see and would never know, but as he turned and exited the pantry, Martha, left momentarily behind, pulled several tissues from her apron and wept until they were wet.

Then she said to herself, just before stepping back out into the real world, "Liar, you'd never leave the man you love no matter what he says. Damn fool!"

* * *

Rejected by Martha, Knowles busied himself with authoring legislation to be taken up by the Senate. On June 16, 1933, the Senate passed the Glass-Steagall Act whereby banks were forbidden from selling stocks and bonds. The Act also created the FDIC, which insures banks against failure. Public trust in banks had to be restored again if America was ever going to recover from the Depression. Glass-Steagall helped engender that trust.

On January 5 of 1934, Al Capone sent for Knowles from prison. Knowles knew what Capone wanted. One month before on December 5, 1933, Prohibition had ended. The Twenty-third Amendment to the U.S. Constitution was passed, repealing the Eighteenth Amendment, which had given the country Prohibition and Al Capone and the Mob.

Knowles departed for the U.S. Penitentiary in Atlanta just two days later. They met in the visitors' area, which was ahead of its time since it allowed the inmates and visitor to share the same table, though never to touch.

Knowles didn't recognize Capone at first. His face and features had aged thirty years, and his croaky voice was that of an old man. Neither man realized Capone was in the first stages of dementia brought on by his syphilis.

They talked; Capone led off. "So, here's my old cellmate, Knowles? Be happy you outgrew these kinds of places," Capone said, waving at the prison's walls, "you wouldn't like it here, and your Uncle Leon wouldn't be able to spring you."

"What? It was you in that cell with me?"

"I would've died without your spoon, Senator. You saved my life. Have you stopped misbehaving now?"

"Yes, I finally outgrew having police officers commit crimes when arresting me. Somehow, that got quite old."

"I know, my old friend. But here I am, a tax cheat indebted to the IRS for two-hundred thou."

Knowles resettled uncomfortably on the steel chair after standing to remove his coat. He laid the coat crosswise on the table. Capone could have reached down and touched it had he wanted. The men had no fear of each other.

"You served on the Task Force that finally got me," the gangster said, "but I need to ask a favor."

Knowles leaned closer. "I'll try. What is it you need?"

"I need to visit my mother's grave in Brooklyn. I need to go there and confess my sins to her."

"What? I would think you'd need a priest for that."

"No, my mother made me promise to never lie to her. And I never have. I don't want to start now. So I need to go there and kneel graveside and tell her my heart."

"Afraid I can't help, Al. I wouldn't even know where to begin."

"Call the warden here in Atlanta. He'll do whatever a U.S. Senator asks him to do. It would only be for a few hours, Senator. Then you can bring me here and toss my sweet ass back in stir until I die. That would be just fine. But first, Brooklyn, please, Brooklyn."

"I'll tell you what I will do. You write it all out in a letter to your ma. I'll personally take that letter to her grave and read it to her. I'll explain you wanted to come but couldn't get away. Won't this work?"

Knowles would later say he'd never thought he would see Al Capone with tears on his cheeks, but that day he did. Huge tears rolled down the gangster's cheeks while he nodded violently and blew his nose on his hands.

"Here," Knowles said, passing him his handkerchief."

"They won't even allow us to have hankies, Senator," Capone said, collecting himself and speaking with a laugh. "God, look what I've become."

"What do you say, Al?"

"I say I'll do it. Tell me where to send my letter."

One month later, Knowles rode the Saturday morning train from Washington to New York, took the subway to Brooklyn and a taxi to the grave of Teresa Raiola Capone.

Starlings shuffled noisily among the surrounding oak trees, while, far removed from human hearing, Knowles read Alphonse Capone's confession to Teresa. The things he had written were enough to see him jailed for three lifetimes.

Still, after the document had been read, Knowles lit it with a book of matches, let it burn down to his fingers, and then crumpled it onto the mother's grave, where it turned to black ash and blew away.

He headed back down the lane toward the waiting taxi.

A flight of starlings burst into the air not ten feet away, sudden enough that most men would have been startled and jumped.

Not so, Knowles Gresham. With measured steps, he continued along to the taxi, climbed into the backseat, and calmly told the driver to drive around.

Then he sat there in the back while the miles rolled by.

"Now I know what happened to the jailer who disappeared," he said to the driver.

"Who?"

"He was a jailer who beat up two young guys with his sap. Almost killed them. Then he disappeared from the face of the earth two weeks later."

"You know where he went?" the driver asked.

But Knowles's racing mind had moved on.

What he had just read had stunned him. There weren't words enough to explain his feelings. But one thing was sure—he would never again approach Martha Bautista with words of love. The world had no more room for even one more sin.

Not after what he had just read.

Chapter 10

Martha's father, who she tearfully said goodbye to when coming to the U.S., was a man named Reynaldo—Rey—Bautista. He was the hardest-working man she would ever know.

At the age of fourteen, Rey Bautista had become a Filipino tobacco farmer a world away from Manila on the island of Luzon. He was a giant kid for just fourteen, broad shoulders with hands capable of efficiently harvesting tobacco leaves in the fields surrounding him for miles in every direction. One day he would happily remember those years, full of smoke and fires from tobacco fields set ablaze to sterilize the soil beneath, making it perfect for planting the light-colored, small-veined tobacco that cigar makers would pay premium money to obtain.

Beginning at the age of fourteen and continuing for the next seventeen years, farmer Rey Bautista woke up at 4 a.m. and worked for the next 14 hours tending tobacco plants in his one-hectare leased plot in the northern Philippine province of La Union. He spent those hours watering, pruning the plants, and caring for each leaf by hand to remove pests.

At harvest time, Rey earned roughly P25,000 ($530) from the sale of tobacco leaves, five months after planting them. It was a small income given the tedious work involved. But for the 31-year old farmer, it was the only way for him to earn a living and feed his four children.

Rey's plight illustrated how the business of tobacco growing hardly benefitted the farmers. Of the P25,000 that he earned during the cropping season that ended in May 1901, about half went to the trader who loaned him the money to buy fertilizer, pesticides, and fuel for the water pump. He netted only P10,000 ($267.62) just barely enough to pay for his children's schooling and food.

Every year, Rey sold his entire harvest to the trader who loaned him the capital on the condition that he would plant tobacco. The second condition was that he sell his tobacco exclusively to the trader. The arrangement left no choice but to sell at a price dictated by the trader. That cycle would be repeated for the rest of his life, Rey knew, bereft of savings, repeatedly borrowing capital from the trader to allow him to plant tobacco. It would be repeated, and his children would know only poverty growing up unless…unless Rey said, "Enough." Which he did, finally, in 1903.

On an October day that year, Rey was visited by the trader, a man named Luis Guyara, who operated out of Makati City. Like Luis, Makati City was wealthy and one of the sixteen cities forming Metro Manila. But way out here, in Luzon, Luis was just like any other person traveling without a bodyguard despite the high crime rate and horror stories of gang-style executions.

Rey would have nothing to do with gangs. He would have nothing to do with violence. But he was willing to make an exception in this one situation, a situation leaving his children always hungry, poorly clothed, with dirt floors in the hovel they called home. Nighttime sleep was almost impossible, so active were the children's head lice as they struggled to sleep. Rey knew the infestation could be traced directly back to the unsanitary living situation, the dirt floors, the lack of running water to clean with. A visit to a doctor for medicine was out of the question. There was no money for such extravagances as medical and dental care.

The situation that begged remedying was this: Rey had been forced to sign a twenty-year contract with Luis. Twenty years of forced poverty and exhaustion just for the honor of all but giving his crop away to the overreaching trader. Rey went to see a lawyer. He was told there was a loophole: the contract was a personal services contract. Only Rey or Luis could perform it. Should either of them die, the deal was no longer valid.

On that October day in 1903, when Luis came to visit, Rey was ready. As the two men walked the fields and discussed Luis's demand for greater production, Rey led them ever farther away from the single dirt road that accessed the field. Finally, at the end of the first row, they came to a recently excavated hole. They stopped and looked down and, just as Luis was turning to ask Rey what the hole was for, his throat was slashed with a tobacco knife. Rey pushed the dying man into the hole and, retrieving his shovel from behind the mound of dirt, began backfilling. The new grave quickly filled with soil. The contract was at an end.

"What choice did I have," Rey said that night to his wife, Questa. "He was starving my family."

The quiet woman, frying bread in the family's sole frying pan, turned and hugged her husband, a rare act, indeed. "There was no choice. If you hadn't murdered him, I would have done it myself sooner or later. We couldn't go on like this. The kids are sick and starving, you work from before sunrise to after sundown, and still, we have nothing but debt to Luis. We will speak of this no more."

A new window was opened on the lives of Bautista family members that day. The new light streaming in and blessing their family was the light of freedom. Rey had never been so blessed in his entire life.

The next tobacco crop was sold on the open market, and Rey pocketed the money, one-hundred-percent his own. He bought shoes for his children, brought home a roast, bought two dresses for Questa, and new work boots for himself. Still, there was enough left over to finance the production of the next crop and keep the family in good stead while the plants germinated and peeked through the rich black earth. Pushing ever-skyward, the billowy leaves would offer the farmer the money crop the earth owed him.

Indoor plumbing was purchased cheaply; a concrete floor was poured in one afternoon. The family felt wealthy beyond anything they'd ever imagined.

And then Rey had his next thought. There was even enough profit left over to lease more farmland. That was it: rent more, earn more. Which he did. And which he repeated over the next several years until Rey moved the offices of his farming empire to Makati City and bought a rambling house—tile floors included—for his kids and grandkids to enjoy.

Eldest daughter, Martha, had already left the family by then to obtain her education in the United States. In fact, she was living in Chicago with Knowles and Natalia Gresham when she received a letter from her father telling her that he was giving each of his children the princely sum of ten-thousand-dollars so they could buy a house for themselves. The year was 1932—a lovely home could be purchased in Chicago for ten-thousand-dollars. But Martha didn't buy. She was consumed with taking care of the Gresham family and the new child, a son, that Knowles and Natalia called their own. How could Martha go off on her own? If she did, she would miss the everyday looking-after of Roland K. Gresham, the new baby boy. The boy with the brown skin and bright gray eyes, eyes like those of his grandfather, the farmer Reynaldo Bautista of Makati City in the Philippines.

Instead, she banked the money. One day she would need it.

Chapter 11

Martha Bautista never told Rey about Roland, her son. Nor did she tell him about Cincy, her daughter.

In 1935 Rey arrived in Chicago for a visit. Martha received a call from Rey at his hotel. Would she meet him for dinner that night at seven o'clock? "I'll be there," she told him. "I'm excited to see you," she said before hanging up.

They met at Hanratty's on Clark Street, a favorite restaurant where it was impossible to get a table without a bribe. But Rey was up to bribery, and he reserved a table in a quiet corner, as far from other diners and traffic as possible.

Rey stood up from the table when Martha arrived, coming straight over to his table, arms outstretched, tears of joy brimming in her eyes.

"Oh"—she wept against his chest, enfolded in his embrace—"I have prayed for you and prayed for you, Papa. I didn't know we would ever meet again on this side."

They sat huddled close together when the waiter arrived for drink orders. They both wanted coffee. Rey reached and took his daughter's hand in his own.

"How is my eldest child?"

"I'm good, Papa. I'm happy."

"Tell me everything, please."

"Well, I live in Washington, D.C. with my employers. They are Knowles and Natalia Gresham. He is the junior senator from Illinois. We spend most our time in Washington."

"But we meet in Chicago. Why is that?"

"The Senate is not in session. At these times, we return to Chicago where Knowles spends his time with the voters. There are meetings and town halls and dinners and lots of speeches."

"He is a very important man, then. That makes me very proud of you."

"Thank you, Papa."

"And what of his wife? You said on the phone that you had to clear it with your patient to come tonight. Tell me about your job."

"Natalia Gresham is a polio victim. She is young and beautiful, and her spirit is the most loving I have ever known. I would do anything for her. Her health is failing, but she continues to fight the effects of her disease. I admire her greatly."

"And so you live with them?"

"Yes, Knowles and Natalia and their two children."

"She could have children?"

Martha took a swallow coffee, cursing the ways of the world that made her lie to her father as she was about to do.

"Yes. Before she became ill. Their names are Roland and Cincy. Roland is the boy, and Cincy is the girl. They are a handful, and when I'm not giving care to Natalia, I'm usually running after those two, but it is a good kind of running after. Like mama did with us."

"Will I meet these people while I'm here?"

"Of course, Papa. We will spend time with them, and you can get to know the family that adopted me."

Coffee arrived, and while her father was ordering, Martha took the opportunity to memorize every detail about him. He was tall for a Filipino, maybe six feet, slender and slightly stooped from all the manual labor he'd done in his lifetime. His features were, of course, Filipino, as were hers, which had her mind racing ahead, groping for the inevitable answer she would have to give about Roland and Cincy, the children who resembled Martha, not Natalia. Of course, they were only half-Filipino, so there was that, but they both had their grandfather's gray eyes, though that was changing daily. Martha and Natalia thought it remarkable that as they grew, their eyes were slowly turning to blue—the same color as Natalia's eyes.

He finished ordering, and it was her turn. She decided on the lobster with au gratin potatoes, green beans, and a small glass of wine.

"Mama couldn't come?" Martha asked once the waiter had disappeared.

"You know Mama. She'll never go more than a mile from home. Of course, Ami still lives at home and refuses to break away from Mama's apron strings. So Mama wouldn't leave her to come here. But she sends her brightest greetings and deepest love to her eldest daughter. She cried at the airport when she said your name, Martha, and knew she wouldn't see you when I did."

"Then I will come to Makati City to see her. Tell her that for me, Papa. Tell her I am coming soon."

"Yes. Now tell me, is there enough money for you?"

"Oh, yes, I am paid very well. Plus, I have free room and board."

"These are tough times in America, this Great Depression. I have worried so often about you."

"No, really, Knowles is paid by the government, and so there's always enough."

Her father nodded approvingly and stirred his coffee refill.

"What about a man for you? Is there someone dear?"

"Not at the moment. There have been men I've dated, but nothing serious. My work is very demanding and, in all honesty, I don't know how I could ever give a man the attention he would deserve. I wouldn't do that to someone right now, Papa."

He sniffed. "So, no grandchildren from my daughter? That makes me sad."

Her heart fell. A great sorrow settled over her as she forced herself to keep still about her children. He would never know.

"Don't be sad. I'm sure it will happen sometime."

"So, there is hope?"

"Papa, there is always hope."

"Now I must ask you one more thing. Mama made me promise to ask."

"Or Course."

"What of this Senator Knowles? Do you have feelings for him? Mama wants to know."

"Senator Gresham? Goodness, no, Papa. I would never do that to dear Natalia. I am the same as you, Papa. I would never do such a thing. How could I ever face you and Mama if I did?"

"Good, good. She will be relieved. As am I. Now, when am I going to come visit at your home?"

"Tomorrow for lunch? Is that good?'

"That is perfect. In the morning I will have time to visit the Exchange and see it in operation. Then I will come to Evanston."

"I'm so excited, Papa. You're going to love my adopted family."

* * *

The Great Depression all but wiped-out Chicago commerce. More than 160 banks in the Chicago area failed, and for the first half of 1935 alone, nearly 7,000 families were evicted.

Jobless men slept along lower Wacker Drive and renamed it the Hoover Hotel in honor of the country's president who had presided over the stock market crash of 1929, until 1933 when FDR took over.

Rey Bautista walked the city streets the morning after dining with Martha, astonished at the suffering he saw everywhere around him. As he walked about before heading up to Evanston, he became increasingly convinced that his daughter must need money. He would delicately approach the subject over lunch and make a plan with her.

The taxi delivered him to the address in Evanston. It was a tasteful, red brick two-story with a chimney at both ends of the roof and two huge oak trees sprawling across the front yard. A circular driveway took him up to the front door, where he got out, paid the taxi driver, and stepped up onto the front porch.

Inside, he was greeted by Martha and the two children, all of whom followed Rey in to meet Natalia. She was as gracious as a person entombed in an iron lung could be, and she turned her face to receive the kiss that the polite Filipino man insisted on planting there. She was happy to meet him, happy to learn about Martha's other family, and she asked him to stay with them, leave the hotel and move there, for the duration of his visit. He refused. Because of time differences, he was up all night conducting business thousands of miles away in Makati City, and he wouldn't bring all that noise and clamor and ringing phones into their home. Next up, Martha took her papa into the kitchen and sat him at the table while she prepared tuna salad sandwiches for everyone. He quietly sipped coffee while she went about her work. Then he said what he'd come to say.

"Chicago is in terrible trouble," he said to her backside. "People are sleeping in the streets."

"Yes, and in October, it can be freezing out. I feel terrible for them."

"The poverty reminds me of my youth on Luzon. It was every bit as bad then, maybe worse."

"I'm sure it was, Papa. I'm sorry you had to endure that."

Thoughts of cutting Luis's throat and pushing him into his makeshift grave flitted across Rey's mind. He winced at the memory, but Martha didn't see.

"I've done very well back home, Martha. I want you to know that."

"I know you have, Papa. Ami has sent me pictures of your home. My goodness, how exquisite!"

"It is a nice place. Mama loves it there. But I need to tell you something about all that."

She turned on her heel, a bread knife in her hand. "What's that?"

"I want you to share equally in my property when I die. Your mama wants that, too."

"That would be very nice." She went back to cutting the sandwiches. "Only let's not talk about that, shall we? That is decades down the road, I'm sure."

He sat back and scratched his head. "Maybe not," he said softly.

Again, she turned around. "Papa?"

"I have the disease people get who smoke. My doctor says it's ironic."

"What, are you telling me you have lung cancer, Papa?"

"Exactly that. They've given me only six months to put my affairs in order. First thing I did was to come here. I couldn't leave this earth without seeing my most precious child again. My eldest child, my second love."

She rushed to her father and bent down to him. Placing her face against his, she embraced him around the neck, patting his shoulders. "Oh-oh-oh—" she was only able to say. There weren't words enough for that moment.

"Yes," he finally said, leaning away from her. "I wanted to say goodbye myself. After I leave here, we won't meet again until the other side."

She stood to face him, her arms crossed. "This is just terrible. Have you thought about American doctors, Papa? We're very advanced here."

"No need. Cancer has spread throughout my body. There's nothing can be done."

"Oh, I am so, so sorry."

She was weeping now, although she tried to shut it off so as not to trouble him.

"So, I am coming to tell you that I am leaving you the bulk of my estate. My business holdings will be turned over to you."

She immediately saw what needed to be done. "It's tradition, father, for the eldest to inherit, and I respect that. But just this once, let's overlook tradition. I want my brothers and sisters—and Mama—to share your property. I'm fine here in America. I have my job, and my nursing license and I will never go without. So please, provide for the others first."

He reached out and took her hand in his. He softly squeezed and let her go. "I thought you might say that, so here's what I want to do. I want to leave your share to the children you're going to have. That will happen after I'm gone. But I'm sure it will happen. I am going to establish a trust fund for your children. My lawyers say this can be done under Filipino law. Your share will be put there. When they reach the age of twenty-one, they will receive their money. Now don't argue with me, daughter. This isn't about you. It's about your children."

Martha's mind was racing. She already had her children, children her father would never know as his grandkids. She suddenly felt horrible for not telling him. Now he would never know. Again, the tears welled up in her eyes. But her loyalty to Knowles and Natalia and their secret prevailed. She kept the truth bottled up inside. Her father would die without knowing about these grandchildren. She was sorry, but it had to be that way.

"If I have children, they will thank you by living up to what you wanted for all of us. That is my solemn promise, Papa."

"That's all I can ask, then, daughter. While we're speaking of these things, I have one question I need to ask you. If I am right in what I say, you can remain silent, and that's my answer. But I can't help but see how the Gresham kids are darker-skinned than their mother. Maybe their father, too, but he isn't home so I can't say about that. Remarkably enough, they also resemble you. Now I'm not going to demand an answer—I have no right. But Mrs. Gresham is confined to her respirator. Is it possible you are the mother of the two children, and you've just forgotten about it?"

She couldn't help but laugh. Deep down, she'd known she would never fool him. But he'd left her a way out. It's just who he was.

"You said, Papa, that I didn't have to answer. Do you like mayonnaise on both slices of the bread with your tuna salad?"

"Yes, mayo on both sides. We'll speak no more of it. But remember, there's a trust for your children. If you only ever produce any."

He was faintly smiling. She knew the look. He'd always allowed his children to have their worlds and their secrets. She loved him and shut off her mind against his sickness and what was coming. She'd enjoy being with him, being his daughter again, as long as possible.

She smiled and tweaked his cheek. "I'll remember, Papa."

"Good. Now let's take our sandwiches in and join your patient while we eat. I want to get to know that woman. She means much to me because she means much to you. Are we ready to move?"

"Let's go visit with her, Papa. You are going to like her very much when you know her better. And she's a wonderful mother."

"I am sure she is a wonderful mother."

"Here we go, then."

Chapter 12

Henry Luce bought *Life* magazine in 1936, and its new editor went to Knowles and Natalia Gresham for a photojournalism story. Knowles was selected because he had been instrumental in passing the FDIC banking laws for consumer protection in 1933. He was, in populist circles, a hero. *Life's* editors thought that his story would blast sales through the roof. Knowles agreed to the article after being hounded by the magazine for over a year. He finally threw up his hands and told his staff to book the magazine's visit to his home in Chicago.

The *Life* staff arrived in the Gresham's circular drive at eight-thirty on a cool June morning. They brought inside too many cameras to count, recorders, and a team consisting of two photographers, three grips, and a writer. If all went well, they expected to have their story and be on their way in just a couple of hours.

Knowles greeted the team in his office on the first floor of his rambling home. He wore a light gray suit and a white shirt with a striped club tie. Martha was nowhere to be seen, and the kids were upstairs in their playroom. At Knowles's invitation, Natalia was their first official stop. Pictures were snapped, and impressions jotted down. Then a writer asked Natalia how old her children were.

"They're very young," Natalia replied in the mirror overhead. "Can we be off the record for a moment?"

"Sure," said the inquiring writer, a young woman barely out of college. Her name was Winona.

"I don't want my children to be part of this."

"Why is that?" asked Winona.

"Because of the crazies in the world outside. It would draw too much attention to them."

"What she's saying," Knowles added, "is we're careful about exposing them to the possibility of harm. It's just better if you mention children but do not portray them with pictures."

"Goodness," said Winona, "my orders are to get pictures of the kids and a cute statement or two. My editor wants them."

"I'm afraid that's not going to happen," Natalia told the young woman.

"But your office agreed to it," she said to Knowles.

"My people might have," he agreed, "but they didn't clear it with me first. I'm saying no, and that's the end of it. Our children won't be part of your story, Miss Graham."

The young woman looked hurt, but that was all part of her journalistic act; Knowles and Natalia knew it. They had talked and prepared themselves for this. They were afraid for the children, it was true, but an even greater concern was the kids' lineage. They bore absolutely no resemblance to Natalia—save for the blue eyes, maybe—and the parents didn't want questions asked by the magazine's readership, especially the senator's sworn enemies. Too many inquiries would come up; it just wasn't going to happen.

Winona took the story in a different direction. "When were you married?"

"That would have been in 1925."

"And when was Natalia stricken with polio," Winona asked Knowles as if Natalia weren't in the room.

"Why don't you tell them about that, honey," Knowles said, referring the question to his wife.

"I contracted polio in 1930."

"So the children were born before 1930?"

"Of course."

"My editor told me there are two children. Is that correct?"

Natalia looked at Knowles. "Correct," came his curt reply.

"And this is 1936, so the youngest of the children is at least seven. Would that be about right?"

Even knowing that Cincy had been born in 1932, Knowles replied that seven-years-of-age was correct.

"And you're sure I can't get a peek at them? What if I look at them without taking pictures? Would that be allowed?"

Knowles felt the anger rise in his chest. Winona Graham was very persistent. "Pesky," was the word of the day for her.

"Again, miss," Knowles said in a low, tight voice, "the kids will not be part of this. Please move on to another topic."

"Let me ask some questions about the FDIC legislation," the other writer interrupted. He sensed that Knowles had reached the end of his patience with Winona and that he was about to ask them all to leave at any moment.

Knowles face relaxed. "Yes, come into our parlor, we'll have some coffee and pastries, and let's talk FDIC legislation. That would be better."

"Nice to meet you, Mrs. Gresham," Winona tossed back over her shoulder as Knowles led them out of her room, down the hall, and into the parlor just off the front entrance. Everyone took a seat. Before Knowles could take drink orders, Winona asked point-blank, "You must have household help, Senator? With a sick wife, two young children, and a constituency in dire need because of the economy, there must be another person or two in the house to help out?"

"Yes," Knowles said, "there is one other."

"What is that person's name?"

Knowles exhaled with a long sigh. She was persistent, beyond anything he had expected, almost as if she were searching for sensationalism.

'Her name is Martha."

"Last name?"

"Why is that important?"

"Our readers always want the full story. The magazine insists on full names."

"Bautista. Her last name is Bautista."

"Might we get a snap or two of her? Maybe a candid shot of her cleaning around your desk while you're sitting there studying a piece of legislation? Our readers love the inside scoop that would represent."

He sighed again, long and hard. "I'll see if she'll agree to that. I can't speak for her, Miss Graham."

"Of course. Is there a restroom on this floor? I'd like to borrow it if I may."

Knowles directed the young woman to the restroom down the hall, then went into the kitchen and asked Martha for help with coffee and pastries. She was ready for that, and everything was prepared.

"How many cups will you be needing?" she asked Knowles.

"Hell, I don't know. Seven. Bring seven."

"Done and done."

Ten minutes later, as Martha was pouring coffee all around, Winona suddenly asked her, "You must have your hands full, nursing Mrs. Gresham and caring for the children as well. Do you live with the family?"

"I do."

"How long has that been the case?"

"I don't recall, exactly. Maybe seven years?"

She looked to Knowles for confirmation. He only shrugged and continued to blow across his coffee.

Winona turned her attention to Knowles. "How long?"

"I couldn't say. Not long enough." He smiled his most attractive campaign smile.

Winona sat back and crossed her arms. She lifted her coffee from the pie crust table and took in a long swallow. She wasn't finished.

* * *

Two weeks later, Knowles received a call from a friend in the Senate. "Congratulations, buddy," said the senator in his hale and hearty voice.

"For what?"

"*Life* magazine. They've got you and your family spread across four full pages."

"Four pages? Seriously?" Knowles couldn't imagine four pages. They hadn't taken enough pictures to fill four pages.

"Yes, and the kids. You've got some nice looking children, Gresh," the caller said. "But they don't look much like Natalia. That's odd."

Knowles felt a cold, icy hand grip his heart. Pictures of the kids? What on earth—?

His administrative assistant returned from the newsstand downstairs fifteen minutes later. Knowles tore the plastic cover off the new *Life* magazine and flipped through to the article.

His heart fell. The *Life* team had taken pictures of the kids as they stood waiting at their school bus stop. The photos were close-ups.

The caption underscored, *Their Little Part-Asian Faces—Natalia Says They're Hers—You Be the Judge!*

He was dialing Henry Luce seconds later.

They had sidestepped him, tricked him, taken pictures of his children even after he'd pointedly refused.

Heads would roll before he was done. Already he was thinking about right-to-privacy legislation. He would author it and present it to the Senate.

Still, deep down he knew the damage was done.

The children in the pictures clearly were not the children of Knowles and Natalia Gresham.

Waiting on the phone, Knowles turned another magazine page. There she was, Martha, her face set opposite the kids' faces on the page. *Does This Look Like Someone's Mother?* the caption asked.

Knowles was ready to strap on his old police revolver and go head-hunting. But he refrained from taking his revenge. It would only serve to draw more attention to the children and their pedigree.

There would be enough of that without his assistance.

Chapter 13

"You better come see, Mr. Gresham."

His eyes opened slowly. Martha was rocking him by the shoulder as he lay snuggled up in his bed in Chicago. Congress was on its Thanksgiving break in 1940, and the Greshams had been back home less than forty-eight hours.

"What time is it?" he asked as he sat up and shook the cobwebs from his head.

"Doesn't matter now. Please, come see."

Knowles threw back the blankets, swung his feet over the side of the bed, and slipped into his slippers and bathrobe.

"It's Mrs. Gresham," said Martha, an ominous tone causing her voice to crack.

"All right. I'll be right there, Martha."

"Come now, please."

He stood up and followed her into Natalia's room.

The iron lung was slowly pumping, its endless whoosh filling the small room. Knowles approached his wife, expecting her to turn her head any second and greet him.

But she didn't.

Her eyes were open, staring straight up at the ceiling. He spoke her name. No response. He lay his hand against her cheek. It was uncharacteristically cold. Natalia's skin was always warm to the touch. But not that morning.

He turned to Martha.

"Is she?"

"She's gone, Mr. Gresham," Martha said, her eyes filling with tears. "I am so sorry."

Knowles's heart broke in two, and he sobbed, touching his lips to his wife's lips, cradling her face in his hands.

"There's no pulse?" he asked, suddenly turning to Martha.

"I've listened several times. She's gone, Mr. Gresham."

"Oh, my God. Bless her soul."

"Yes, God bless her sweet, sweet soul."

"We better call someone, Martha."

"I already have. Haver's Funeral Home is sending someone."

He could've guessed that. Arrangements with Haver's had been made long ago. He was relieved by the foresight. He was going to need his wits about him as he told the children and prepared for their grief. It was going to take everything he had to pull them through this terrible loss.

Then he stopped, ashamed at what he was feeling besides his loss. He was also feeling relief. The worst had finally happened. He would no longer spend his days and nights in dread of Natalia's passing. Almost immediately he was scolding himself for thinking like that. He told himself that what he was feeling was nothing less than evil. Better men would buck up and remain faithful to their wives. But Knowles wasn't a better man; he had to admit. Her death was a relief, plain and simple. Of course, he would never tell that to anyone. It was a secret he would always carry, one for which he would forever be apologizing to Natalia's spirit.

He sat slowly in his chair beside her. He studied her beautiful face, painful as it was to imagine her gone, never to smile at him again. It was a wonder how much he had experienced from just her face and voice. He'd maintained an entire relationship—such as it was—with her face and voice alone. Human adaptation is bottomless, he realized, marveling at what he'd become, what she'd become.

But it was over now. She was gone, and he was alone with their children.

And with Martha. What would become of Martha now that she was no longer needed to provide medical care? His mind raced as he considered. The kids were in school all day, and after-school childcare would be much less expensive than the full-time nursing care Martha brought to the household. He realized he didn't want to think about all that just then. He needed time to process, time to get past the enormous hole in his heart left there by Natalia's death. But the time would come for him and Martha to talk; that was inevitable.

He shivered, thinking he wasn't yet as alone as he was going to be when Martha left them. His shoulders shook, and the tears ran down his face. Martha came up to him and pulled his face against her hip. She shushed him and ran her fingers through his hair. He immediately felt less afraid of the future. He realized that all was well as long as Martha was close to him. What did that mean? Had he transferred his needs from Natalia to Martha? Now his shoulders shook with the heartbreak of his loss, and he turned against the nurse's body. He couldn't help himself, then.

Couldn't stop the feelings.

He wanted more of her. The line that had existed between them was gone.

He felt disloyal to Natalia, now unmoving, an arm's length away in the stilled respirator. But he had to be honest with himself.

He wanted more.

* * *

In the months to come, Knowles spent as much time as possible with Roland and Cincy. The children missed their mother terribly, which was, at bottom, gratifying to Knowles because of the peculiar way they'd had her in their lives. They had never told their father how difficult it was all those years, knowing their mother would never hold them or dress them or tend to their childhood bumps and scrapes. She was, as the children knew her, just a voice and a smiling face. They loved her, of course; rather, they loved what they had of her.

Moreover, there was no denying as they got older that they didn't much resemble their mother. She was very pale and delicate, with a light complexion and flaxen hair, whereas they were brown-skinned and sturdy with coal black hair. Admitting to no one they looked more like Martha than their mother, the children tried to ignore the fact. When they were just into their teens, however, Roland one day expressed to Cincy his belief they were Martha's children. Cincy responded by throwing an empty bottle of Coca-Cola at Roland, which caught him just above the jaw, splitting his lip and requiring stitches at the hospital. Neither child would confide in Knowles what had prompted Cincy's outburst, and he eventually stopped asking. Whatever it was had passed since the duo was talking again and joking back and forth like before.

Nights were the worst for Knowles. He was accustomed to sleeping alone, of course. But he was also accustomed to arising at any time during the night and taking a particularly challenging work problem to Natalia. She had been forever awake and there to talk.

In those dark hours, their initial discussion would inevitably lapse into their love for each other, and they would admit how much they missed holding each other while bitterly complaining about how unfair life had treated Natalia. Knowles couldn't help but repeat how much he wished it had been him the polio had chosen to victimize in the Gresham family. But Natalia wouldn't hear of it. The people of the country needed in Congress a man of Knowles's decency and work at improving the lives of all Americans. Polio, she argued, had done the people of America a favor by taking captive the non-contributor under the roof. She was able to tell this to Knowles matter-0f-factly as if reading him a recipe. But deep down he heard in her voice the regret and sorrow living inside her. He knew Natalia better than she would ever realize.

Gone were those nights spent with Natalia, those nights he treasured. Now, Knowles spent his middle-of-the-night wrestling matches with his demons alone. Several times he was ready to go down the hall to knock on Martha's door and ask if she would come to the family room and talk with him. But he never knocked. It would place him in the role of the employer who tried to take advantage of a female employee for sexual favors. Because, deep down, he didn't want just the late-night talks from Martha. He wanted her flesh, too. And he felt like she still craved his in return. He even anticipated, at times, that she would come creeping into his bedroom, remove her nightgown, and climb into bed with him. He imagined holding the covers up off her as she slid her body across the bed where, that night, flesh could know flesh. Knowles burned for Martha those nights.

But one thing was true through it all: he felt guilty for his lust and desire, felt like he was cheating on Natalia, and redoubled his efforts to hold his unserviceable urges tamped down. There might be no returning if he ever allowed that base part of his makeup out of the bottle. That would surely be the end of the arrangement.

This life of yearning without fulfillment would end in the next few months when Martha would finally leave Knowles and the children to begin a new life with a new patient because that was her calling.

Then his most desired object would be gone from view, if not gone from his heart.

It was a time he would delay as long as possible.

Chapter 14

Knowles and Martha found they were in love before she left home. It was four months after Natalia died that the husband and nurse ended up in bed together.

Two months later, on April's Fool's Day, 1941, Knowles brought home a box of chocolates and a bouquet of twelve red roses. Proudly bearing his gifts, he found her in her bedroom, packing clothes into a suitcase. He immediately forgot all the words he'd been rehearsing to tell her. The open suitcases felt like two stones that had been dropped on him. He stared, speechless, stunned. He immediately thought he had overstepped and run her off.

He finally managed to start the conversation. "What—what's this, then?"

She looked up, taking the flowers and candy from him. Turning away and setting them aside on her chest-of-drawers, she turned back to face him. "It's my mother. She's very sick. Ami called me. I'm going home to take care of her. She needs a nurse, and I can do that."

"But what about us?" Knowles blurted out, voicing what had gone unsaid up to then.

Her eyes narrowed at him. "What about us? I didn't know there was an 'us.' We've had our times together, we've shared a certain kind of love, Knowles, but there is no us. Not in a long-term sense like I need."

"But there can be! Let me show you how it can work."

"Maybe. But first, I must take care of my sick mother. That's my job. You desire me; she needs me. It's a simple choice."

That afternoon, she flew from Chicago to Los Angeles where, three days later, she boarded a ship bound for the Philippines.

Eighteen days later, her ship arrived in Manila. She then made her way to Makati City. Manila was called the Pearl of the Orient, an elegant city with broad, tree-shaded boulevards. Makati City was an extension of the capital, the wealthiest city in the country. She found her mother and set about taking care of her. But it didn't last.

On Jan. 2, 1942, the first Japanese soldiers arrived in Manila and then Makati City. Thousands of civilians were rounded up, told to pack food and clothes for three days, then taken to the University of Santo Tomas in the heart of Manila where they were held for the next three years. The prisoners included executives of U.S. companies, ship passengers, diplomats, journalists and Martha and her mother, and Ami, her youngest sister.

In March 1944, they were taken to a prison camp in Santo Tomas, each carrying a suitcase containing their meager belongings.

Martha, Questa, and Ami followed the camp's daily routine with the rest of the prisoners. The 6 a.m. and 6 p.m. roll calls; the bowing to the Japanese sentries; unsatisfactory meals of watery lugao; and the rare joy of finding a piece of water buffalo hide hidden inside the gruel.

The world's first kamikaze pilot took off from nearby Mabalacat East Air Field in October 1944. It was a desperate time for the Japanese military, and desperate times called for desperate measures. The kamikaze pilots were but boys and were mostly unskilled pilots who were taught to takeoff—but not to land. They performed as expected and died the deaths of heroes, crashing insanely into the sides and top decks of American warships. Thousands of Americans died from such attacks. To the Japanese commanders, it was more than a fair trade—one kamikaze pilot for hundreds of American sailors and soldiers. The Japanese were emboldened and began training the young pilots en masse, their complete training only three weeks in total.

After the invasion of Manila in 1942, the Americans had surrendered, and the Japanese had rounded up the defeated soldiers. They were weak and starving, but their captors gave them no food or water. Instead, they force-marched 70,000 Americans and Filipinos 55 miles up the peninsula in the tropical heat. Martha, her sister, and mother were included in the ranks of the marchers. Thousands died on the way.

It was a cattle drive out there, going up one side of the road, the Japanese coming down the other, lots of times swinging their clubs, hitting as many Americans and Filipino civilians as they could. Filipino soldiers were primarily spared since they were to be used like dray animals in the prison camps, building lean-tos, digging sanitation ditches, and clearing the jungle for airfields. Thousands of Filipino soldiers died at the hands of the invaders as they followed their terrible orders.

At the town of San Fernando at the head of the peninsula, the prisoners were packed into stifling, steamy train cars and shuttled to Capas, where they were forced to march seven more miles to Camp O'Donnell.

When the prisoners arrived at the camp, there was no food and no medicine. Hundreds had fallen ill along the way. The prisoners begged their captors for something to eat. They were ignored. The prisoners were left to die in the concentration camp.

1,600 Filipino civilians died in the first 40 days at Camp O'Donnell. Survivors were transferred several months later to Cabanatuan, a former Army supply base about 25 miles east.

At Cabanatuan, the Japanese soldiers sorted out the most attractive of all the women. Martha was one of those chosen. Then began the violations. Night after night, the unlucky women were passed amongst the soldiers, who raped and beat them without letup. Days were spent in agony from the pain of sexual assault and beatings with fists and boots. Then night would come again—always too soon—and there was no sleep as they were abused yet again and again. Many of the women became pregnant.

As if that weren't hell enough, the officers at the base learned Martha was a nurse. They had a use for a nurse.

The Imperial Army had long wanted a weapon of mass destruction it could use against the American Army. They were never able to unlock the secrets of nuclear fission, for which the American government gave thanks to their judicious God. So the Japanese scientists kept looking. Commanding officers at Filipino internment camps were given orders to undertake to develop chemical weapons of mass destruction and were ordered to use the prisoners as guinea pigs for their experiments.

Martha was taken aside one day and assigned to a new Quonset hut. At the rear of the hut, where she would now spend her days, was a crude laboratory. Use it, she was commanded, to develop anthrax. The Imperial Army had decided only a weapon such as airborne anthrax could stop the Allies from invading Japan. The pressure was there to produce the spore and weaponize it.

Would Martha comply with the order? Would she work on such a horror as a chemical weapon? She did, for they were ingenious manipulators, using whatever a prisoner held dear to get results. Whatever they wanted, she told them, she would do. In return, they agreed to cease raping and beating Ami and cease forcing the old women, including her mother, to stand outside unprotected when the monsoons came. Many had died of pneumonia; Martha was terrified her mother would be next. Thus, when she was offered protection for her family in return for anthrax, she jumped at the opportunity.

Her resources included access to a small medical library at the prison. She learned that the organism *Bacillus anthraces* caused anthrax. In some parts of the world, this could be found in cattle or other hooved mammals. It was infrequent in western Europe and the U.S. but easily discovered and isolated in animals in Asia and Africa.

Martha knew nothing about finding and cultivating anthrax. So, she read everything she could about the organism and discussed it at length with the Japanese officers who were in charge of deciding whether she lived or died. All around her others were dying, men and women who had come to the camp with her and after she was already there. But Martha survived.

One day, she began to see how her situation could be used to help others. They delivered 100 Petri dishes to her lab at her request. The Petri dishes had to be filled with growing evidence of spore production. Now she needed proof her efforts were on the right path. So Martha read new publications and reread some more. Eventually, she told the guards she needed bread, many loaves of bread. By dawn the next morning, she had her bread: seven loaves, still warm from the oven. Martha had learned from her studies that once the starches in bread began to set up, it became a tempting treat for hungry mold spores. Because molds do not have chlorophyll like other plants, they are particularly aggressive feeders, so thousands of spores could cover a piece of bread overnight and millions in a few days. Martha was an almost-overnight success. She told the officers she was very close to producing anthrax in her lab. She said maybe she even had it already. All she needed were guinea pigs—human guinea pigs—for testing.

The soldiers separated five of the unhealthiest prisoners and sent them to Martha's lab for testing. When backs were turned, and Martha was left to her research, she took to feeding the daily bread to the guinea pigs. Within weeks, rib cages began disappearing as weight was added to the bones of the five. Martha then told her captors she needed other everyday items: she required beef, she required poultry, and much more. The search for the evanescent spores was fully underway. After all, the soldiers told one another, look at all the spores in her lab. She must be very close.

Martha, meanwhile, was feeding her experiments beef and poultry. Now the captives that had once been the sickest of all prisoners were beginning to radiate good health. And more, they looked like some of the healthiest of all the base's habitués.

Martha's experiments widened in scope, and her needs for animal flesh increased. Under orders from Emperor Hirohito himself, the soldiers plied her with everything she requested, hoping against hope they would be the ones to announce they had isolated and reproduced the deadly anthrax spores.

Masks and gowns were required. Soldiers were fearful of entering her laboratory and all of its white and green growing things. They stayed away except to deliver her the refrigerator she needed to preserve her cultures and human foodstuff.

Martha spent the rest of the war at the base. In return, she thrived and essentially was given whatever she needed to hurry along her quest, including new prisoners for new experiments. She kept the churn going, switching prisoners in and out, feeding as many as possible and then seeking out a new group from among the sickest on the base. It wasn't much she was able to provide, but it kept many alive.

Chapter 15

The Americans began taking back the Pacific, winning such monumental battles as Coral Sea and Midway before finally wading ashore in the Philippines in October 1944. MacArthur started to stage daring rescues at the prison camps. First at Cabanatuan on January 31, 1945, then at Manila's Santo Tomas.

At 9 p.m. Feb. 3, 1945, an American tank, the *Georgia Peach*, crashed into the front gate. "Are you Americans?" a soldier shouted to the skinny prisoners who swarmed around the mechanized cavalry. "Yes!" they yelled back.

"And what of you?" the soldiers demanded of rag-tag Filipinos. "Friend or Foe?" It was almost impossible for the Americans to tell enemy from friendly because so many of the Japanese soldiers ripped away their clothing to pose as prisoners. But the American commanders weren't buying it. If a "prisoner" wasn't starved-looking, they weren't friendlies. Thousands were captured in this manner and hauled off to American prisons.

After liberating the camp, the Army used Santo Tomas as its headquarters. One day, as Martha was in the courtyard about to accept some chocolate from a soldier, a mortar shell exploded. Shrapnel hit her in the jaw; she could still open her mouth but only partway. The soldier was killed.

After the nuclear bombing of Nagasaki, the Japanese Empire fell.

Questa died shortly after liberation when her body could no longer process solid foods. She weighed sixty-five pounds at her death. Martha, who was all but American after so many years in Chicago, left the islands soon after, zigzagging across the Pacific to avoid detection of still-roaming Japanese ships. Ami didn't travel across the Pacific with her sister, returning instead to Makati City where she undertook the management of what was left of the tobacco empire their father had built. It would take months before it was productive again and financially stable. There was no time to waste.

A full month later, Martha's ship arrived in Long Beach, and she caught the first plane eastbound to Chicago. Her focus was only on Knowles and her children, Roland and Cincy.

The taxi dropped her at the top of the circle drive in front of Knowles' house. She didn't know whether she would find him there or in Washington, but Chicago was on the way to the east coast, so she tried there first. She would have telephoned, but the senator's home numbers were all unlisted. She tried calling his Washington office but was turned away as just another Filipino ex-prisoner-of-war seeking assistance the senator was unable to provide. When she told the woman she was a personal friend of the senator's, the line went dead. She didn't bother calling again. The war had touched America, too, Martha thought. What was once a small town, Washington DC had now become a suspicious crush of lobbyists and lawyers and harried congressmen. The friendly town she'd once known had evaporated.

Martha walked up to the front door of the Chicago home and rang the bell. She heard the chimes sing out inside. No answer, however, so she pressed the button a second time.

This time a young woman, who Martha judged was perhaps ten years younger than Martha, answered. Her lithe body filled the doorway as she leaned forward, smiling.

"Would you tell Knowles that Martha is here?"

"Martha?" said the young woman. "Martha Bautista?"

Martha's heart swelled in relief. At last, she was someone to someone in America.

"Yes, I'm Martha Bautista."

The young woman extended her hand. "Well, I'm Janice. Yes, Knowles is here, and I know he'd be delighted to see you. Won't you come in? Bring your suitcases, please."

Martha placed her luggage inside the door and closed the familiar stained glass behind her. She inhaled a deep breath. It smelled exactly like she had dreamed in all her years of captivity. It hadn't changed.

Janice led her into the parlor. The furniture had changed. What was once brown and out-of-fashion was now remarkably light, pastel in color, and expensive-looking.

"Please, have a seat."

Martha sat down in the middle of one of two couches and smoothed her dress over her knees. Her heart was pounding wildly in her chest as she waited on the man she loved, the man she had dreamed about every night for over four years of literal hell. At times, his face and memories of his body were the only things she had to hold onto. Now she was about to be rewarded for her steadfast hold on their memories.

Then he was there, coming into the room, arms outstretched, tears filling his eyes. He encircled her with his arms, and she pressed her face into his starched white shirt and club tie.

"You came back," he whispered at the top of her head. "I thought you were dead when I didn't hear all those years. I sent a captain of the army looking for you. He reported back that you had died during the march out of Manila. Oh, Martha! Oh!"

She didn't move. She only clung to the man she loved and sobbed quietly into his chest.

Then he pulled back. She noticed for the first time that Janice had left the room. A feeling of sudden fright gripped her bowels. She could feel the fear all the way down to her toes as a light began to turn on inside her head.

"Janice—she's your—she's your—"

"Janice is my wife, Martha. I thought I'd lost you all those years ago. I'm so, so sorry, but I was wrong. I would have waited, you know?"

"I did wait," she managed to mutter. "I waited all those years. It never occurred to me that—that—"

"You never had a thought that I would marry? It was so hard with just the kids and me after you left. I'm sorry, so sorry. But good news! Janice and I have a son. Isn't that wonderful?"

"Oh?"

"The wonderful part is that we named him Cleveland Bautista Gresham in your memory. Now just to hear his full name will break my heart. Oh, my dear God."

"I need to go," Martha said and stood upright.

"No, you need to see your children. You must stay here and get to know your children. Please, Martha."

"They're your children now, Knowles. I'm sure they know Janice as their mother. She seems like a kind woman, and I'm sure she's taken them on as her own. They needed that after their mother passed away. I'm glad for your children, Knowles. You've done well by them."

But her heart was breaking. She was fighting for air to breathe. Hurrying into the foyer, she clutched her suitcases and tossed a request over her shoulder that Knowles call a taxi.

He hesitated, and she could see that he was still in shock and had no response to the turn his life had just taken. Maybe there wasn't an appropriate response; she didn't know.

He went into the kitchen where the phone was connected and dialed for a taxi. Then he hurried back to the front door to make arrangements with Martha. She feared he would ask her to stay on and become part of the family. She knew that was impossible. She would never agree. Neither would Janice. There would be no satisfaction. Only heartbreak.

In the backseat of the taxicab, Martha took inventory. Her disfigured jaw was throbbing; her heart was barely able to keep her alive, broken as it was; she was penniless except for the phone call she could make to Ami. Once the request had been made, she knew she would suddenly find herself showered in American dollars. Still, she had no plan. So she did the next thing in front of her. She had the taxi drop her at a hospital where she knew they were looking for nurses. They also offered room and board to the nursing staff. It was all she could conceive of doing that afternoon in Chicago.

Wearily, she lugged her suitcases through the hospital's front doors. Two hours later, she was being shown to her new room in the nurses' quarters. It was Spartan: a bed, a wardrobe, a sink, a percolator on the ledge of the one window, and a stack of bedding. There was nothing else.

She needed nothing else. In the camps, she'd learned to have no needs. Lessons that would serve her well going forward.

She closed the door, pushed her suitcases into place with her feet, and sat back on the bed. Then the tears came, the heart-wrenching flow of tears that lasted well into the night. When they finally eased sometime after midnight, she spread her blanket across her exhausted body and slept until dawn when her first shift at the hospital would begin.

She would be working the surgical ward. It would be mind-numbing, thankless work changing dressings and cleaning up after the very ill. It was exactly what she needed just then, work that would insulate her mind from her wounds.

She rolled over in bed and opened her eyes.

No tears came out.

They wouldn't ever come again, either. Not for Knowles, not for her children, and certainly not for herself.

Imprisonment had taught her to let go of everything a person could ever hold dear. It was time to dress in her hospital whites, settle the nurse's cap on her head, and report to the charge nurse.

She stood up and stretched.

Who? She asked herself. Who should she long for?

There was no one left. There was only the moment and, of course, there was only the sick and dying people who needed her touch.

So it was that Martha reported on the second floor of the hospital that morning in Chicago.

An hour later, the entire heartbreaking history was fading from her mind.

Giving of herself to stay alive was working.

She was home.

Chapter 16

Growing up and watching his politician father deal with dozens of needy people every day, Cleveland B. Gresham knew he wanted nothing to do with politics when he came of age. He would find another way to support himself and the family he imagined he would head one day.

Cleveland grew up primarily in Chicago with his mother, Janice, who abhorred Washington and its phoniness, so she stayed home in Chicago whenever his father, Knowles, journeyed to Washington to work. First came college at the University of Chicago. His sophomore year, he fell in love with a girl named Wendell. They married the following summer and almost immediately had a son. They named him Michael. After graduation, Cleveland entered law school, again enrolling at the University of Chicago.

Roland and Cincy, Cleveland's half-brother and sister, were also settling in the Chicago area, and the three were together every night of the week at one another's apartments. They cooked Italian, ordered in Chinese, watched Laugh-In on TV, attended Bulls and Bears events, and generally had a great time.

But then the war in Vietnam kicked into high gear. Cleveland was drafted just out of law school and was inducted into the Army where he was assigned to JAG—Judge Advocate General's—duty. He served in-country in Vietnam and later served at Fort Bliss. Both assignments were prosecuting criminal cases under the Uniform Code of Military Justice.

Cleveland became quite good at prosecuting. When his tour was up, he returned to Chicago and began looking for work. The Cook County State's Attorney's Office was actively recruiting ex-JAG officers, so Cleveland said why not? He started working there and immediately loved his job. He planned on staying a long time.

Cleveland became very adept, and very talented, at sending criminals to prison. He became known among the defense bar as the state's attorney you prayed you didn't draw on your new criminal case. If you did, your unfortunate client was looking at a case that probably wouldn't settle with a friendly plea bargain, probably would go to trial and probably would result in a full-term prison sentence.

Wendell, Cleveland's wife, finished university and began her student teaching. She was happy with her work and was a dutiful and loving mother to Michael, a happy, inquisitive five-year-old with a penchant for schoolyard sports.

After securing a full-time position as an elementary school teacher, Wendell met and fell in love with a student, age ten, who was bouncing in and out of foster care, a little boy whose psychiatric treatment suffered from the instability of his living situation. Wendell made inquiries into Arnold's legal status, put in a request with the Bureau of Children's Services, and Arnold found himself moved into the home of Wendell and Cleveland Gresham, his new parents.

Arnold—Arnie—and Michael became inseparable. During the long winter months in Chicago, they played outdoors for an hour then came inside for two hours to warm up, and then back out. This went on through all the endless months of winter.

Their childhood consisted of board games, card games, sewing superhero costumes to wear, building elaborate spaceships out of cardboard, all interspersed with TV shows for kids and movies every Saturday with their dad.

Meanwhile, the boys' father rose within the ranks of State's Attorney's Office.

Chapter 17

In November 1966, in a city known for shocking crimes, the most infamous crime of all occurred. It happened Thanksgiving Night when a deckhand from New Orleans, who'd come off a boat in Chicago and was looking for work, decided it would be amusing to kill someone. The union hall had no work for him that first night, so he went drinking and carousing down along the waterfront. His name: Richard Dotty.

Dotty staggered out of the last tavern that would serve him at two a.m. Looking for a place to sleep away his intoxication, someplace close to the waterfront, he spotted a two-story building across from a hospital. He tried the front doors of the building, but they were locked. So he went around to the alley and crept up to the fire escape. Dotty was a tall man, and with the help of a fifty-five-gallon drum, he managed to reach up just high enough to touch the bottommost section of the fire escape. Grasping it with both hands, he pulled mightily. Then he fell off the drum, righted it, and climbed back on and pulled again on the fire escape's bottom section. This time, the cantilevered ladder responded by promptly unfolding down to ground level, waiting there to allow firefighters to enter the building or for second-story occupants to descend.

Dotty stepped from the barrel over onto the first section of the fire escape. Then he began drunkenly climbing, managing to ascend to the second-floor landing where he could look inside two side-by-side windows. Both were dark. He peered inside, his forehead pressed against the glass. Neither window allowed much of a view other than inky, middle-of-the-night shapes. He tried sliding them open, but they wouldn't budge. He figured they were probably painted shut and locked from the inside. Then he noticed a third window, this one to the right of the fire escape. This window was cracked an inch to allow fresh air to enter.

Ever so slowly, ever so quietly, Dotty slipped his fingers through the opening and began lifting upward. The window slid up noiselessly and easily. When it was fully open, he stepped inside. He didn't know where he was; didn't know who, if anyone, was there in the room with him, so he waited for his eyes to adjust to the pitch black of the room. Slowly, a bunk bed took shape on his left, and then one on his right, four beds in all. He listened for the sounds of sleep and was rewarded with the knowledge that all four beds were occupied.

Dotty crept to the door, which was already open. He stepped into the hallway and looked right and left. Nondescript, except for more doors, two open on his left, one open on his right and one closed farther down. Ever so softly, masking the sounds of creaking floorboards, he made his way down to the door at his left. He withdrew his deckhand's blade from its scabbard on his belt and entered the room. Two beds, one right, one left.

Now his eyes were fully adjusted to the dark. Add to that a pale cast of moonlight filtering inside as the moon had escaped the cloud cover and now appeared in the heavens in full glow. Intoxicated and walking like a silverback ape, Richard Dotty made his way to the first sleeping body. He leaned down and had himself a closer look. A woman, young, maybe mid-twenties, sleeping on her back, her mouth partway open. He could hear the air whistle in her nostrils as he drew the knife blade across her throat and covered her mouth with his free hand while she died. He then turned and crept to the bed opposite, where he repeated the same slice-and-silence murder of yet another young woman.

Had there been more light, he would have noticed one repeating feature inside the room: both wardrobes, right and left, were filled with nurses' dresses on the hangers and white nurses' shoes below, for Dotty had invaded a dormitory where the hospital's student nurses were housed.

But he didn't notice the dresses, and he wouldn't have cared even if he had. Circling back into the hallway, Dotty crept to the next room and entered. Only two of the four beds were occupied as the two who were missing were inside the hospital where they were working the night shift. Dotty's blade flashed in the moonlight as he took the lives of two more student nurses, both females, both sleeping soundly in happy anticipation of the next day's hospital shift doing the work they loved. He had now killed six young women.

He returned to the room where he'd entered, crept back inside, and was slicing the throat of his seventh victim, when she was able to force her mouth out from under his hand and cry out, "Aggggh!" Dotty continued the deep cut then abruptly came upright. In the noise and haste, he hadn't heard the lower bunk behind him creak as its occupant stole from the bed and immediately slid beneath it onto the floor.

She held her breath and waited there as a loud outcry erupted in the room from the other occupants, now coming awake in response to their roommate's crying-out. Steady and sure of his goal, Dotty managed to fight them down one-by-one and kill each one while the others waited, frozen in their beds with fear. Now he had killed nine nurses in all. When he had finished, he stood upright. The one bed was empty.

Beneath the bed, Martha Bautista shivered and shook, holding her breath, praying. The man didn't sense that she was there and of course wouldn't have known she was serving as the director of nursing for this clutch of students, including living amongst them while they studied and worked through their hospital rotations. But he didn't need to know all of this: if he had heard her, he would've flipped the bed aside and taken her life, too.

Martha closed her eyes and slowly inhaled through her nose. She twitched as the man's boots shuffled up alongside her bunk. Suddenly a light was switched on in the hallway. The man must have relieved his bloodlust at that point. Back through the window, he lurched where he double-timed down the fire escape. Left behind and crying tears of horror, Martha slowly came out from under the bed, switched on the room light, and looked on the bloodbath the intruder had left behind.

Lying flat on the bunk above Martha was a twenty-four-year-old student nurse. She was gasping her final breath. Martha threw her arms around the girl and whispered to her. The girl's eyes glassed over and became fixed, then she was gone. Still, Martha kept whispering into the girl's ear in the hope that the last words she heard would be the message Martha had for her. The girl's name was Nettie, and she was gone. Her death caused Martha to shatter inside.

She screamed, ran from the room, turned and ran down to her right, and shattered the glass cover of the fire alarm. Quickly grasping the exposed handle of the alarm, she jerked it downward and crumpled to her knees with relief when she heard the sudden wail of the siren throughout the dormitory building. She struggled back onto her feet.

Martha then ran room to room, doing quick examinations of each young body lying immersed in its blood, hoping against hope to find someone living to whom she could give aid. But she found no one. Dotty had terminated the lives of every young woman on her floor—except for her, of course.

Finally, the police dashed up the inside stairs, into the hallway where Martha stood frozen against the wall, having lapsed into shock. She couldn't speak; neither could she move. The police officers ran beyond her with guns drawn, turning on lights and scouting for the intruder. But he wasn't to be found.

Next came the detectives. They wanted to talk to Martha right then and there, no waiting.

"Yes, I got a look at him—sort of a look," she told the detectives.

"Tell us what you saw."

"It was a man; he was wearing boots. I could see his boots under the bed."

"What else?"

"I saw the knife with its curved blade dangling from his left hand."

"Tell us about the knife."

"It was—it was too dark. But there was one other thing I saw."

"What was that? Quickly now!"

"He didn't have a ring finger on his left hand. It was gone."

"How much of it was gone?"

"All of it was gone, clear down to the first joint."

Soon after, when Martha had been led downstairs and deposited inside an empty bedroom on the first floor, Cleveland Gresham arrived on the scene. He was the on-call state's attorney that night. Upon receiving a call at home, Cleveland had leaped from his bed, dressed, and hurried outside into the waiting police car, which then ran under sirens and lights, taking the prosecutor to the horrendous scene so that he could offer whatever legal help the investigators might need.

Cleveland was stunned. He'd never imagined a murder scene as horrific as this one, and it caused him almost to break down. There was blood everywhere, including in the hallway where the first responders had tracked it as they ran room-to-room searching for survivors. There were none, of course, and now the medical personnel had cleared out so the Chicago PD Crime Scene techs could do their investigation and preservation. The techs from four police districts were soon working side-by-side to capture every potential piece of evidence and to preserve the crime scene by measurements, photographs, and notes.

The investigation of the scene took forty-eight hours. During this time, the entire building was emptied and the nurses, including Martha, moved to another dormitory building. Cleveland saw the survivors' board and realized Martha Bautista was in the mix. Martha had been a legend in the Gresham household when Cleveland was growing up. He sought her out and sat for an hour with his arm around her shoulders while she rocked forward and back, over and over, weeping about Nettie, who Cleveland assumed was her student.

The hospital hired armed guards—off-duty police—and positioned them throughout the student dorms and the hospital itself. The entire campus took on a wartime aura as uniforms and guns were at every turn. Everyone was a suspect; no one came or went without full photo IDs on display.

The media was having a field day. Sensationalism ran rampant. TV news and print journalists scrounged every last possible bit of story from the scene and the dorm's occupants, regardless of their actual proximity to the crime or its investigation. Then the police released a drawing developed from Martha's description of the four-fingered left hand of the killer.

The press began referring to the crime as "Nine Fingers." The moniker caught on; even the prosecutors and police started using the phrase. Nine Fingers was rampant on page one of America's newspapers and was the subject of weekend news for weeks. Then the case began fading from the front page and TV screens until, without warning, a Wacker Street mime walked into the East Side Police Station and reported seeing a man with four fingers on his left-hand jump onto a barge. Detectives were alerted and headed for the river. Shipping companies were questioned, dispatchers were queried, and union halls were interrogated. But no one saw or heard of any such worker. Sure, they guessed it was entirely possible there were river workers missing digits from traumatic amputations; boats are dangerous places. In fact, there should be lots of those. But specifically, someone missing a left-hand ring finger? No simple answers came because nobody kept track of this kind of stuff. Alerts were sent to all boat captains to review their crews. The man had to be found before he struck again. Still, sixty days later, there was no sighting aboard the boats. At long last, the police decided the mime was just plain mistaken or lying.

Baffled, the cops gave up on the lead and moved along to the next case.

Chapter 18

Sobering up the morning after he'd murdered seven student nurses, Dotty panicked. He knew the police were searching for the killer. On the other hand, he was reasonably confident they had neither a description nor a name to identify him. He also knew the police would have all points of exit from the city under surveillance night and day. He knew to avoid airports, bus stations, and the trains at Union Station. Men intent on suddenly leaving the area would be profiled and stopped at all such transportation hubs.

So, Dotty used his head and his union card. The card was his ticket out of Chicago. Within hours of the murders, Dotty was employed by Empire Barge Lines departing Chicago, dispatched to haul soybeans south from the granaries. Twelve hours later, Dotty began feeling some relief while, twelve hours back north, the Chicago PD and the FBI were running out of ideas for making an arrest. They felt outsmarted, yet they weren't ready to give up, far from it. If their subject was patiently waiting to leave town, they could be patient, too.

Working on the barge, Dotty kept to himself. No one knew his real name. Even his union card was a forgery, an identity stolen from a friend who'd been washed overboard off the coast of South Carolina when his ore ship failed to avoid a devastating ten-year storm. Dotty had broken into the dead friend's apartment, raped and murdered his widow, and stole his papers, passport, and ID.

The burglary had empowered him. The old Richard Dotty was left out there in the ether somewhere, while the new Richard Dotty, traveling under a false name, was being given a second chance at life. His old sins and crimes were erased. Dotty could attribute most of his life's failings to his drink, but there was nothing he could do about it. Nor did he want to. His vice was like a wild horse kept locked away and only taken out to be ridden when the moment was perfect.

Dotty made his way to New Orleans on the barges, then found his way onto a freighter bound for Panama. At that time in his life, he couldn't get far enough away from Chicago.

But with each passing mile, as they steamed ever south, Dotty found he was breathing easier. At long last, they entered the Panama Canal, and Dotty knew he was free.

Chapter 19

Martha was suffering even more than the night of the murders. Her situation would one day be known as PTSD, but in her generation, the syndrome hadn't yet been named. Her doctor sent her to a psychiatrist when the anxiety pills stopped working. The psychiatrist was a kindly, older woman, who held Martha's hand and told her she would help her recover. The doctor called it a nervous breakdown. More pills, more talking therapy, and Martha wasn't one tick better than when she began.

Knowles heard about her narrow escape and called her. He asked how she was doing, and so, having nothing left to lose, she told him. She was exhausted, histrionic, half-mad, she said. She went for weeks without sleep; food more often than not wouldn't stay down; and she was afraid of city pedestrian traffic and large groups. Knowles listened, heard her out, and told her she needed people in her life who she could trust.

Then there was a dead silence between them as they processed this comment. But then Knowles explained what he'd meant—she needed to see her kids, Roland and Cincy, who Martha had assiduously avoided seeing. It wouldn't have been fair to Knowles or Natalia if the kids discovered her true identity, so she merely made sure that wouldn't happen by staying away.

But then Knowles helped her—when she was at wit's end and ready to take her own life— by calling Roland and Cincy. He told them the woman who nursed them and took care of them during early childhood was Martha Bautista. He wanted the kids to get to know her and include her in family events. Which both Roland and Cincy undertook to do. Just as Cincy had realized before, it was quite obvious they looked much more like Martha than they ever had Natalia, their mother. Roland saw but didn't see, according to Cincy. She guessed he didn't want to look closer.

But Cincy decided she wouldn't dwell on it. She became very close to Martha in time. One night, after a pre-Christmas dinner with Martha, Cincy, a bit heady on delicious white wine, almost asked Martha who she was to them, but she resisted. Although, with the wine onboard, she finally admitted to herself that their history was other than what she'd been led to believe by her father. She resented that, but there was no solution. What was done was done. Later that night, Cincy came awake with tears in her eyes. In her dream, she had been speaking with her mother. And her mother looked precisely like Martha.

For Martha, coming into contact with the children who were her offspring was thrilling. Thrilling, and, even more, it started healing her. Some nights she was able to sleep for two or three hours—more than she had since the murders. Even happier-making, the hole in her heart was slowly closing up. She was healing from her abandonment by Knowles. She believed, for the first time since returning from the Philippines in 1945, that she was going to have a better life than ever. Her children were everything to her. They always had been; she could never say it out loud. But now she could. Even if only to herself.

Chapter 20

Cincy was a bright child, a little girl who preferred a new microscope for Christmas, passing her time examining skin cells or pond water while the new Shirley Temple Doll sat idle.

Cincy grew into a tall, skinny young woman who worked in her father's Senate office during her high school summers. Upon graduation, she was accepted to Columbia University where she studied biology. Her goal was to write for *Scientific American* and various medical journals, which she eventually got to do.

But after a few years, she began feeling unchallenged and burned-out. So she looked into medical school, made an application, and was accepted into the University of Illinois Medical College. She focused her electives on community health and family medicine with an eye to practicing medicine at an inner-city clinic. When asked by her father why, she said, "Because that's where you'll find the real diseases." Then, in a spirit of equanimity, she added, "The poor, especially, need and deserve the best medical care America can offer."

Senator Gresham approved and encouraged Cincy to make her dreams happen. He was proud of his daughter. Martha was beside herself with joy when Cincy was admitted to medical school to become a doctor. It seemed the next logical step for a child of hers—especially the female child—and made her very happy, very proud.

Roland was teaching civics in a local high school, raising his two young sons, and enjoying the Cubs and the Bears. He took his boys to all the games. Soon they were wearing the shirts and caps of their favorite Chicago teams. He had been a reticent child, maybe even a bit troubled, so when he started teaching and growing a family, Martha was glad for him—and a little relieved. Normal meant everything when it came to her kids.

Chapter 21

When Cincy graduated medical school, she began working at a walk-in medical clinic in Southwest Chicago. She would often bring her young nephew, Michael Gresham, to work with her. While his aunt met patients and prescribed medications, young Michael would sit in the clinic lab and, like his aunt before him, while away the hours with a microscope that revealed a whole new world. On alternate days, Michael accompanied his father to his law office on LaSalle Street. He had left the State's Attorney's Office sometime after the slaughter of the student nurses, unable to take much more of the crime he confronted seven days a week, counting on-call days.

Cincy married a clinic doctor, and they bought a downtown condo two miles from the Loop, where they made their home. In 1975, Cincy learned she was pregnant, almost an impossibility for a forty-three-year-old woman by natural means. When she gave birth to Lester Havilland, she had just turned forty-four.

But there was a problem from the outset. Lester was stuck in the birth canal for forty-five minutes, became anoxic, and suffered brain damage. He was jaundiced, and his Apgar was off the charts. Nobody had to tell Cincy what a problem she had just brought into the world in the sense of a lifetime of care and medical attention for her baby boy.

The medical attention was easy enough; doctors were abundant in Cincy's world. But the caregiving was an insurmountable problem. She would be in her middle sixties when Lester turned twenty, and not long after, when she was retired and living on a budget, Lester's need for hands-on care—bathing, toilet, meals—would still be ongoing, and the expense of providing for it would skyrocket.

So, Cincy did the next best thing and paid a visit to Cleveland in his law office. They hugged, always happy to see each other, and Cleveland could feel the bunched-up muscles in her back and shoulders. The new burden of the unwell baby was wearing her down.

Nevertheless, they sat and made small talk. Suddenly, though, Cincy broke down weeping.

"This is about Lester, I believe," Cleveland said. "I think I understand."

"It is about Lester. He needs so much more than I can give. So much more than we can afford."

"Who was the doctor who delivered him?"

"Randy O'Connell. He's a great guy. Very busy, but a great guy."

"Was there anything unusual about the delivery?"

"Lester was breech."

"Bottom-first."

"Exactly. Then Randy couldn't get him turned. It seemed like it took forever, and I was finally exhausted and couldn't push anymore."

"Well, Cincy, I don't have to tell you that remaining in the birth canal for too long can be catastrophic. The contractions can compress the head, oxygen is shut off—a quick mess, and you're off to the races."

"All true in my case, according to the records."

"Plus, you got exhausted. Damn, Cincy."

"I was in labor nearly thirty hours, Cleve."

"So we have some things to look at."

"To be honest, I've talked to Randy about all this. He's of the opinion it was simply unavoidable due to the breech."

"What about you, Cincy? What's your opinion?"

"Whatever else happened, the delivery was allowed to go on too long."

"What about your pelvis? Had Randy seen any sizing problems?"

She shrugged. "It's normal size. Nobody ever said anything different."

"Have you looked at other possible causes of Lester's deficit?"

"No disease, took all prenatal vitamins, no smoking, no alcohol. Good genetics. The birth caused it."

"What do you want me to do, Cincy? I know you didn't come here just for a shoulder to cry on. What's your plan going forward?"

She shivered, though it was warm in the office. "Randy tells me his office manager allowed his malpractice insurance to lapse. A total oversight and she was fired for it. For what good that does me. He's judgment-proof just like the rest of us, with our school loans and such. He probably still owes half a million to the government. I know I do. Which I'll never get paid off now. Not with the costs of caring for Lester shredding our budget every month."

"How are you holding up personally?"

"Omigod. He cries nonstop day and night."

Tears flooded Cincy's eyes and streamed down her cheeks. Lawyers keep Kleenex tissues on their desk. She plucked two from the box and started dabbing. But still, the tears came. It was evident to Cleveland that his half-sister was exhausted. She had gone as far as she could go without help, without at least some hope.

Just then, the office door creaked open, and Michael crept into his father's office, ready for his afternoon work. He paused and hugged his aunt before sitting down beside her in the second visitor's chair across from his dad.

"Hey, Michael," said Cincy. She blew her nose and managed a smile. "Ready to help your aunt's case?"

"I am," said Michael. "What kind of case is it?"

"We're discussing the possibility of a medical malpractice case against the doctor who delivered Lester. But there's a problem. The doctor has no med-mal insurance."

Michael looked at his father and shrugged. "So why not sue the hospital? They've got coverage."

"Sue them for what, son?" Cleveland said.

"I don't know. Failure to properly monitor the birth. Failure to provide adequate personnel, or properly trained personnel?" He turned to his aunt. "What was the problem?"

"Too long in the birth canal."

"Sue for failure to monitor fetal heart tones. Juries love that one, according to the cases I've read."

Cincy's eyes rounded. "You're reading law cases?"

"Sure. Why not?"

"Talk about precocious."

"It's what they pay me for around here. I write briefs and motions."

"At fourteen?"

Michael smiled at his aunt and placed his hand on her shoulder. "Aunt Cincy, the cases are written in English by judges who put their trousers on one leg at a time, just like me. Why wouldn't I read them?"

"I'm just surprised, that's all. And proud of you, Michael."

Cleveland placed his elbows on his desk with folded hands. "Okay, I like Michael's failure-to-monitor theory of recovery. I was going to suggest the same thing. And more."

"Here's another angle, Dad, Aunt Cincy. If the doctor didn't have med-mal coverage, there's a reason behind that. I'd find out why he didn't have it and, if it slipped off someone's radar to pay the bill, I'd look at who placed that employee in the doctor's office. There might be a possibility of going after a headhunter for failure to adequately train and supervise an employee. At least look at that and try to find the doc some insurance coverage."

Cincy said to her half-brother, "I like this Michael guy. He's been doing a little scut work for me, but he belongs here. The kid's a natural lawyer."

Michael's father nodded his agreement. "I couldn't have said it better. My boy."

Michael threw up his hands. "Just doing my job. That's why they pay me two-fifty an hour."

"Hey, it's 1976. Consider yourself well-paid."

"Just kidding, Dad."

After they broke up, Michael headed for the law library, his make-shift office. He lifted the ivory desk phone from its cradle and dialed for information. Once he had Dr. Randy O'Connell's office on the line, he made an appointment for two days hence. He was going to meet with Dr. O'Connell before the firm filed suit against him.

Two days later, Michael and Dr. O'Connell met in the latter's office on Clark Street.

"I was expecting someone older," said the doctor, barely suppressing a smile. But he held out his hand to Michael, who shook it gravely.

Michael wasn't smiling. "I'm the one you want to talk to, Dr. O'Connell because I'm the one who will be drawing up the lawsuit against you if we have to sue for my Aunt Cincy's baby."

The doctor blanched. He shook his head and had trouble meeting Michael's gaze. "Yes, that." He motioned for Michael to take a seat and followed suit when the young man sat. "I told Cincy that my medical malpractice insurance was allowed to lapse. Otherwise, I'd be helping her to make a claim against my carrier. I feel horrible about it, Michael."

"I'm sure you must. But I'm not here to threaten you, doctor. I'm here to help you."

"Help me?"

"Yes. I'm looking at other claims that could be made in your case. Specifically, I'm looking at claims you might be able to make against third parties."

"I don't follow."

"Well, look, doc. What's the name of the employee who let your insurance coverage lapse?"

"Elin Tanner. A nice, older woman with three kids to feed. I liked her."

"How did she come to be working here? Did you hire her from an agency?"

"Matter of fact, I did. Our normal office manager was seriously hurt in a car crash. I needed someone to take over immediately. So I called Sundy Temps."

"Sundy Temps? They're in Chicago?" Michael pulled out a small spiral notepad and jotted the name down.

"Sure, the largest employment agency around. They're who we always use."

"Hmm. I'll just bet they have errors and omissions insurance."

"What's errors and omissions insurance?"

"It's like medical malpractice, but it's for malpractice that a business might commit."

The doctor leaned back in his chair and drummed his fingers on the desk. "Tell the truth, Michael, you've lost me here."

"Well, think about it like this. When you call a temp agency for help, you have the right to believe you're calling an expert. Someone who has proficiency in matching a worker with your needs. Follow me now?"

"So you're going to say they were negligent because they sent someone who wasn't trained to manage office insurance policies?"

"Right."

"They should have sent someone who'd keep my insurance in force?"

"Bingo! That is exactly what I'm saying."

"Jesus. I like that, Michael. Who came up with this idea?"

Michael smiled. "You're looking at him."

"Okay, so what do we do?"

"Well, I make a claim against you, and you hire a lawyer. He and I then put our heads together and figure out a way for him to file a third-party complaint against Sundy Temps. It's that simple."

"Because Sundy Temps has its own insurance?"

"Exactly."

"Michael, that's genius."

"Not really. It's how lawyers think."

"How would you know that?"

"Because I'm going to be a lawyer someday."

"I'm loving this. I haven't been able to sleep at night. You're saving my life."

"I hope it works out that way. We can only try."

"What if it doesn't work out that way?"

Michael's eyes narrowed. "Then I sue you and come after you tooth and tong. I won't let go until you either pay my aunt or file bankruptcy. It won't be pretty."

"God. Sorry I asked."

"No, you need to know. I'm not here on a fool's errand, Dr. O'Connell. My aunt and Lester are going to get the help they need. I promised them."

"Then let's get to it, Michael."

"I already am."

Chapter 22

Increasingly aggressive like his father, Michael pushed ahead the effort to make Cincy whole. His next stop was Sundy Temps.

"My father is looking to hire a new office manager. Can you help with that?" Michael asked an employment counselor named Gina. Her nameplate above her blouse pocket said, *Hi, I'm Gina! Can Sundy Temps Help?*

"Sure we can," Gina said through her Juicy Fruit. She snapped, then snapped it again.

"We need someone to manage our law office. Do you have managers with that kind of experience?"

"Why, of course. Male or female?"

"It doesn't matter."

"Would you like me to send a few for interviews?"

"Yes, we'd like that. But promise me this—you'll send only the best you have. Three of them."

"Done and done. I can have them there this afternoon. First one at three o'clock? Does that work?"

"Yes, then three-thirty and four."

"Done. Now, let me get some particulars. What's your name again?"

"Michael Gresham."

"The name of the company?"

"Gresham, Sachs, Scarlatti, and Prosy. We're a law firm. We'd prefer someone well-versed in insurance issues."

"Let me note that. Insurance issues. Got it." She scribbled on a yellow legal pad in front of her, only two words. *Insurance work.* "Do you have a card?"

"I do. Here we go."

She took the card and studied it. "So you're on LaSalle?"

"Yes, we are."

"You're an employee there? Oh, I get it. Your dad is the Gresham, and you're Michael

Gresham."

"Correct. Be sure now. Insurance training."

"Not to worry."

Fanny L. Mystal was the first candidate through the door that afternoon. Michael, working out of his dad's office while he was away in court, stood to meet and greet. After shaking hands, he motioned Ms. Mystal to have a seat.

"Gina faxed me your resume, Ms. Mystal."

"Fanny, please."

"I'm interviewing several candidates this afternoon. For me to tell everyone apart after you're gone, I'd like to record the interviews. Is that all right with you if I record what we say back and forth today?"

"Sure. That would be fine, I'm certain."

Michael reached over and clicked the Sony recorder's red button. The tape began turning. Then he turned his attention to the candidate, Fanny Mystal. He said, "We particularly need someone well-versed in insurance policy management. Would that be you?"

She answered his question with one of her own. "Insurance policy? Like insurance on cars?"

"No, like malpractice insurance for doctors and lawyers."

"Oh, golly. I don't know much about that."

"That's okay. Tell me what you do know."

"That's just it. I don't know anything about malpractice insurance."

"You do know how to manage insurance policies for your employer?"

"Sure do."

"Tell me the steps that would take."

"Well, I'd put all the insurance policies in one folder, and I'd mark it *Insurance*. Then I'd file it under the I's."

"So far, so good. What else would you do, Ms. Mystal?"

"If anyone needed to see the file, I'd pull it and take it to them."

"What else would the office manager do about those insurance policies?"

"I can't think what else. Just knowing where they are. That's very valuable right there."

"Have you ever managed your employer's insurance policies before?"

"I must have." She tapped a ruby-nailed finger against her lips. "I'm thinking. Can we skip that and come back?"

"Sure. You're Sundy Temp's top candidate for law firm office management?"

Fanny L. Mystal smiled. She was somewhat embarrassed. "That's what Gina told me to tell you."

"Gina told you to tell me you're the best? Does Sundy Temps test its candidates for knowledge about a specific area of work?"

"Not that I know of. I wasn't tested."

"What made Gina think you're the best qualified?"

"Darned if I know. Should we call her?"

"Not just yet. Let me circle back. Have you ever managed an employer's insurance policies before?"

"You know, I'm blanking on that."

"Meaning you can't think of any jobs like that?"

"Right. That's right for now. I'll keep thinking, though."

"Now let me back up and ask the same question a little differently. Ready?"

"Ready."

"If you came to work here—or anywhere, for that matter—would Sundy Temps have insurance on you in case you messed up?"

"Gina tells everyone to admit nothing if someone says we screwed up. She said to sit quietly and take notes but don't answer any accusations. That's good enough for me."

"But what about insurance coverage on you?"

"That's the whole point, Mr. Gresham. Gina said their insurance company would come running in case we screw up, but we're not allowed to discuss it with our employer at all. Not ever."

"So there is insurance covering you?"

"Oh, yes."

"Have you ever seen the policy covering you?"

"Not—no. I don't work at the Sundy office. They send me out on jobs."

"But Gina has for sure told you there's insurance on you?"

"Definitely. But she says it won't be any good if we cooperate with the enemy."

"She used those words? 'Cooperate with the enemy?'"

"Same words, yes."

"Who would the enemy be?"

"Why, that would be anyone I was working for."

"Your employer is the enemy?"

"That's how she said it. I don't agree with her, but who am I? I only work there."

"Sure, I understand. Anything else you want to tell me about it?"

Fanny smiled and put her face in her hands. "I shouldn't."

"Shouldn't what, Fanny? You shouldn't what?"

"I shouldn't ask you this. But I want to. Did Elin work here?"

"Elin Tanner? She worked for Dr. O'Connell."

"She got fired because she didn't pay the insurance policy?"

"How do you know that, Fanny?"

Fanny took her hands away from her face. She looked up at the ceiling and kicked her feet. "I shouldn't say this but oh, well. Elin said she forgot to pay the insurance policy when it came due. She's worried about getting sued. Are you going to sue her, Mr. Gresham?"

"I can't answer that right now. Why would it make a difference to you?"

"Honestly, I need this job. It wouldn't matter to me if you sued her. It's not like she's family or best friends—nothing like that."

"Well, I'll keep you posted. How about that?"

"That's very fair. Thank you."

"Do you have any questions for me?"

Fanny went to shake her head "no" but stopped just before. "Would I be managing insurance policies if I worked here?"

"You would, yes."

"Would you train me how to do it?"

"I thought you already knew. I told Gina I need only candidates who understand how to maintain office insurance policies. Isn't that why you're here?"

The air went out of Fanny. "No, I'm here because Gina said we need to score this job. There's rent to be paid."

"She told you she needed to pay her office rent and so she needed you to snag our job?"

"Yes. Am I in trouble, by the way?"

"Not at all. You're not in any trouble, I promise you."

"I won't have to come to court?"

"We might need you to testify, yes. But we don't know about that yet."

"Oh."

Michael then terminated the interview, gave his thanks to Fanny L. Mystal, and walked her out the door. He canceled the next two appointments. He canceled because he didn't want to create an interview where the candidate did, in fact, have insurance experience and did, in fact, answer the insurance questions correctly. Let Sundy create that self-serving testimony if they wanted to. Michael wasn't about to do it for them.

Later that day, he played the Fanny recording for his father. When the tape shut off, Cleveland shook his head. "Just unbelievable, these people. No wonder Dr. O'Connell's insurance policy didn't get paid."

"I know. So how about I meet with Dr. O'Connell's lawyers, and we go after Sundy Temps?"

His father stood and reached across the desk. He indicated he wanted to shake Michael's hand. So they shook.

"Well done, son. Damn well done."

Michael grinned. "We aim to please. Isn't that the firm motto?"

"It soon will be, Michael, if it isn't already."

The conversation then drifted off in the direction of the Chicago Bulls' basketball playoffs. Father and son would be attending the games together.

That night at dinner, Cleveland couldn't stop talking about Michael.

Michael went to bed on a full stomach and a kind of excitement he would feel for years after. The excitement that came from doing the right thing.

Michael was doing the right thing, and it sat well with him.

Then he slept a long, peaceful sleep, dreaming of cross-examining negligent doctors and hospitals.

He loved cross-examination done right.

Only done right.

Chapter 23

Michael's mother was Wendell Gresham, a woman who taught Latin and Calculus at Hoover High in the suburbs. Michael happened to study both subjects under his mother while attending HH.

On Good Friday of his senior year in high school, before noon, Michael dropped by his mother's classroom, for it was her free hour and he knew he'd find her grading papers. He knocked on the door jamb before entering.

Wendy Gresham, M.A., was a study in educational professionalism. She'd earned her master's at Loyola University in high school education with certificate endorsements in Latin and mathematics. She was a quick learner in both areas, Phi Beta Kappa out of Loyola, and she expected Michael likewise to excel. She saw no reason why he wouldn't.

Wendy was a woman with a quick smile if a student deserved it but a piercing gaze if the moment—errant student, for example—warranted. She was friendly to all students but played no favorites, although the very bright ones tempted her to gravitate their way. She made a practice of never grading her students on the curve. She graded them only against themselves, looking just for improvement in their knowledge and understanding from the first day of the term to the last. If there was a marked improvement, the student was rewarded with an A grade even though, had they been graded on a curve against the rest of the classroom, they would've received at best a C minus. Thus, students known as kids who were challenged in languages or math would find themselves bringing home report cards with A's in Latin and math to their parents. Many conversations between parents and Wendy took place each semester when Wendy, in those moments of irony, tried to explain how their child was doing so well in Wendy's class.

But that's just how it was. She played fair, and she expected you to play fair. She passed this attitude onto Michael. He grew up willing to abide only open and honest transactions between people. But he was nobody's fool. His mother was quick to crack the whip on those who tried to use her, and Michael grew up with the same sharp eye out.

That Good Friday, however, his heart was heavy as he entered Wendy's classroom.

"Hey, Tiger," she said without looking up from the papers she was inking in red, "how's it going?"

He let out a long sigh and sat in the student chair facing her desk. "I'm confused, tell the truth."

"Aren't we all? What about?"

"It's Jane Sullivan. She wants us to get married before college."

Wendy's head jerked up. "Come again?"

Michael smiled his best smile. "Thought that would get your attention. No, seriously, we've been pretty close, Mom, me and Jane."

Wendy's eyes narrowed. "Close in what sense?"

"Well, we've been intimate."

"Michael—I warned you about this."

"I know, I know."

"What did I tell you?"

"You told me to use protection if I ever found myself in a situation like this one."

"Well? Have you? Are you?"

"Yes and no."

"What the hell does 'yes and no' mean?"

"The first time we—you know—I didn't have anything with me. I never in my wildest dreams ever thought Jane would go all the way."

"Were you pressuring her?"

He slouched in his chair. "Maybe a little. Yeah, some."

"That's normal for boys your age. Did she refuse and you forced her?"

"Never, mom! You know me better than that! Why'd you say that?"

She pointed the blunt end of her red ballpoint at him. "Because I need to have the facts. All of them."

"We both agreed to everything. I was shocked."

"I'm sure you were. Here's the deal, Michael. There are always going to be women who will try to trap guys like you. Maybe by having sex, maybe by getting pregnant. You're a good-looking kid, and you're smart like your mom and dad. You want my advice?"

"Yes, I do."

"Keep your dick in your pants."

"I knew I shouldn't have come in here. Jeez."

"You have a better way of handling your teenage lust?"

"I—no."

"Then do as I say. Use the zipper on your pants for what it was made for. To keep you in and them out."

"I thought it was made for peeing."

"That's a bonus feature, Michael. The real use is for you to avoid getting trapped. All boys need to hear this."

"Curious, Mom. Do girls get this speech, too?"

"They should. I don't know. I don't have any daughters."

"But you were a girl. What did your mom tell you?"

"She told me if I didn't make straight A's in high school, she'd jerk out my arms and beat me with the bloody stumps."

"That sounds exactly like Grandma Rollins."

"Sure is. You always know where you stand with your grandma."

"Okay, let me make sure I've got this right. Keep my zipper up and make straight A's. So far I'm hitting on all cylinders, Mom. I'm four-point-oh in school, and my zipper is—"

"Your zipper damn well better be closed. Remember the bloody stumps, Michael. You get someone knocked up, and I'm sending Big Tony after you. Got it?"

"Got it."

"Now get out of here and let me finish grading these exams before my one o'clock. It was a good talk."

"Good talk, Mom."

* * *

The Monday after the zipper talk, Cincy received her check for ten-point-five million dollars. The hospital and Sundy Temps had each agreed to pay one-half of the total cost of providing lifetime care for Lester, a sum of ten-point-five million dollars. But the money hadn't just fallen off a tree. It was the result of two painful years of litigation. At last, the defining moment came when, just as the parties were having their settlement conference with the judge, Sundy Temps admitted it had negligently provided an employee to Dr. O'Connell, and she had allowed his malpractice insurance to lapse.

Sundy admitted its fault because Cleveland Gresham had the tape made by his son, Michael, in which Fanny Mystal nailed her employer. In full settlement of Dr. O'Connell's claim against Sundy, Sundy's insurance carrier agreed to pay one-half of what Dr. O'Connell owed to Cincy and Lester for negligently managing Lester's birth. Cincy celebrated with Lester and the other Greshams that night. She showed up at the house, driving a blue MG sports car.

"You didn't wait long to waste money on the car," Cleveland exclaimed to his half-sister when they had an alone moment.

"Don't be stupid, Cleve. That car isn't for me."

"Then who?"

"I got it for Michael. He earned it in Lester's case."

"I gave him a bonus of a hundred dollars, Cincy."

"I figured as much. Well, I'm giving him the car. Don't get in my way."

That autumn, Michael showed up on the University of Chicago campus, where he was now enrolled, driving a powder blue MG with the top down. He was proud of the car, and it certainly stirred all the coeds to give him the eye as he drove through campus.

But Michael wasn't buying what they were selling. Not yet.

The zipper was to keep in what shouldn't be out.

And you didn't need to know Latin or Calculus to figure that out.

MICHAEL

Chapter 24

MICHAEL

Arnold Gresham—Arnie—my older brother, deserves a place of honor in this retelling. He is critical to my story, and my life does have its lighter moments. They say a lot about Arnie, who's always been an important character in my life.

The night I graduated from law school, my father took me for a ride in his Cadillac. We stopped for cheeseburgers and onion rings, swung down to Wrigley Field and saw the lights, then slowly drove back up along Lake Michigan, looking for the lights of ships somewhere beyond our world. My Dad—Cleveland Gresham—was never a real talkative guy, especially with Arnie and me.

Arnie was a problem child from early on. I was the healthy one, but dad treated us as equals, much to his credit, especially given how difficult it must have been raising Arnie with all of his problems versus me, who was reasonably independent and low maintenance. I remember going as a family to Arnie's psychologist when I was quite young. We sat for what seemed like forever in her office, the grown-ups talking while Arnie and I sat beside each other on a loveseat, playing kick the other guy when no one was watching. My mom cried a lot during those sessions. My dad kept one arm around her, hugging her close every time she'd break down. He'd pull her up snug to his side and offer her another handful of Kleenex. That's the way they spent a lot of time when they were figuring what should come next with Arnie. Mildly put, he was one hell of a handful.

Anyway, that same night I graduated from law school, Arnie had insisted he would show up for the ceremony only if he got to drive my dad's MG to the auditorium. Mom was in bed with the flu, so it was just the three of us: Dad and me in the Caddy, Arnie bringing up the rear in Dad's prized sports car, a Brooklands Green-over-Black 1965 MGB Roadster. That car would be worth $35,000 today, restored. I don't know what it cost my dad new back in 1965.

After the ceremony, I was approached by Bill Howerton, my best friend in law school. Bill needed a ride home. Arnie spoke right up that Bill could ride with him. My dad was slow to agree but finally, unwilling to embarrass Arnie, he gave him a thumbs-up. Arnie and Bill left the parking lot before dad and I were even loaded back into the Caddy. That was the last we'd see of Arnie, or Bill, that night. The Infamous Arnie Night.

When I graduated, we were living in Barrington, a horsey area maybe twenty miles due west of downtown Chicago. We had the typical house and five acres, plus a stable and chicken coop (mom lived for farm-fresh eggs). We were very happy living there, the four of us.

Dad was still working long hours at the law office, and on top of Mom's teaching, she was also everything else: homemaker, livestock engineer—meaning she kept our two horses watered and hayed, and all-around household organizer.

Arnie was practicing law with a downtown silk stocking firm where, much to my amazement, he was excelling. He was a great lawyer and would one day rise to the top of the four-hundred-lawyer firm's litigation group. As for me, it was all about girls and college, most of the time in that order.

My undergraduate degree was a double major: accounting and English. My first two years undergrad I took all the accounting courses our university had to offer; my last two years I took all the American literature courses they could serve up in those scant twenty-four months. From Hawthorne to Hemingway, Updike to Irving (John, not Washington), I was your boy. I was also a pretty fair forensic accountant, which would stand me in good stead all through my life as a lawyer.

So here is what happened the night I graduated law school, now that you have a bit of background, a feel for who our family was, and your first inkling of why it's important to know we lived on a hobby farm. Which also had its own ancient Ford tractor. Three of our five acres were hay, so we mowed with that tractor and then hooked up the manure spreader and went back over the same tracks.

Arnie decided to take a detour to Bill Howerton's apartment where he lived with his cousin, a night shift employee at the local 7-Eleven. Driving west on the Kennedy, they pulled off at the cousin's store and picked up a case of Bud. Why a whole case? Why is the sky blue? I'm sure I don't know.

They killed two beers at the 7-Eleven while Bill shot the bull with his cousin, and Arnie sat on an upside-down milk crate, thumbing through the latest Playboy before inching it back inside its plastic cover. Meanwhile, outside at the curb, as close as it could be parked to the doors of the

7-Eleven, sat the green/black 1965 MGB. It was a beautiful car; customers coming and going stopped to give it the once-over. They nodded with approval before climbing back inside their jalopies and heading home. Or wherever.

By the time they left the store, Arnie and Bill were working on their third beers. They did not attempt to dispose of the open cans of alcohol before they pulled out into traffic, a clear disregard for the law prohibiting open alcohol.

Two miles south of Barrington was the Olde Orchard Kountry Klub. The OOKK was a privately-owned short-nine course built by the loving hands of a bunch of residents who, before the city sprawl set in, lived a good ten miles from the nearest golf course. They wanted to play, so they built their own. Sand and sod, the basis for the nine greens, were lovingly trucked in and shoveled into place by the board of directors. The fairways were plowed up and rolled down by Willard Rench, the local who owned the Firestone Store and had access to a highway roller. Two ponds were dug out—one on the second fairway, and one on the seventh—by the same man who dug wells in the area, with the aid of a huge backhoe and a dump truck. He drilled two wells and installed a circulation system that would guarantee the water holes never fell below the water table. Areas of rough were planted alongside the fairways with a different breed of thick prairie grass. Hit into that rough, and good luck making it onto the green in regulation. So it went. When all was said and done, after two years of labor and investment in materials and machines, OOKK opened up to its members. It wasn't a public course, members only. Which had always rankled my brother Arnie because the Greshams weren't members. Our dad thought it too expensive to join, and he considered golf a wasteful pastime anyway. Quail and deer season--those were more his style. But not Arnie. Arnie had been the number five man on the high school golf team and thought himself deserving of membership in OOKK, but dad wasn't springing for it.

Back to the MGB and Arnie and Bill.

They left the freeway at Barrington Road and headed south toward Bill's apartment rather than north toward our home. My dad and I had been home, served some soup to mom, and were relaxing with the ten o'clock news at the same time that Arnie, suddenly inspired, whipped the MGB into a hard left-hand turn, shot across the OOKK parking lot, bounced through a short line of bushes, and raced up the number nine fairway, outbound toward the number eight green.

"Holy shit!" Bill cried out when he realized where they were. By now, the joint adventurers were on their fifth beers and pretty much pain-free.

"Whazzup?" said Arnie as he guided the car onto the eighth green, flattening the flag, and whipping the steering wheel all the way to the right. He cut a considerable donut in the putting surface. This was the same green—one of nine—that the OOKK members had tended and planted while on their hands and knees during that first year of construction. Now it was ruined, an angry set of sports car tire tracks cut an inch into the surface. Talk about repairing your ball mark. Anyway.

Here they came, roaring off of eight, a hard left then rolling onto the number seven fairway, which was a par three with a waterhole down the hill. Then the boys were climbing up and coming down that hill, hitting the water at full speed, probably a good 30 MPH, shooting ten feet out from shore and submerging the MGB, the 1965 with the green-over-black paint job. Arnie, just drunk enough, was incensed at the car for its sudden refusal to start right back up. In water up to his waist, still arranged in the driver's seat, he repeatedly turned the key and hit the starter in a dozen vain attempts to get the vehicle moving again.

Bill waded around the car and laid his hands on Arnie's shoulder. "C'mon, asshole," Bill said between clenched teeth, "we've got a mess here."

Arnie looked up and seemed to come out of his haze just long enough to understand their predicament. Always the lawyer, Arnie's first thought was to remove all evidence of who had driven on the course. He looked up at Bill in the bright moonlight. "Not to worry, William. We'll hike out to my house and fire up the Ford tractor. Then we'll come back here and drag the MG out with a chain. Simple as shit, my boy."

Bill was just far enough gone that he agreed to Arnie's plan. For the rest of his life, Bill would kick himself for not telling Arnie to go to hell and just hiking on home since he had had nothing to do with the driving and intention to create the mess. But he didn't hike home; he hiked the opposite direction with Arnie. When they arrived back at our farm, it was 3:30 a.m.

The keys were always in the tractor. You didn't dare remove them or dad would kick your ass if he wanted to drive it and found the keys missing. It was an unwritten rule. So the tractor grumbled awake when Arnie turned the key. "C'mon!" he yelled at Bill, standing helplessly nearby. Bill, resigned to a life of shame by now, climbed up onto the tractor and sat his butt down on the flare of the Ford's fender. He rode sideways while Arnie guided them all the way back to the OOKK. Of course, the tractor had no headlights, but that didn't matter to the bandits. The moonlight was more than enough to find their way.

Directly through the parking lot, Arnie drove again, this time heading across the rough and circling the water feature on the seventh. Arnie was almost surprised to see the MGB hadn't moved. Undiscovered, he set about pulling the car from the water. He had Bill jump down and unwrap the chain from the PTO on the back of the tractor where it hung coiled. Bill did as he was told and fastened the chain to the front end of the tractor then waded into the water, fell to his knees, and attached the chain to the little car's rear undercarriage. When all was ready, he raised his hand and gave Arnie the "Back up!" hand signal. Arnie instantly hit the gas, and the tractor roared.

Except he hadn't shifted into reverse. Blame it on the beer.

The tractor leaped across the lip of the waterhole, jumped off the bank, and shot far enough into the water that it slammed into the rear end of the car. "No problem" yelled Arnie to Bill. "I'll just whip her into reverse."

Which he did. After that, the tractor's wheels spun and the vehicle buried itself in the mud clear up to its hubs. Try as he might, Arnie couldn't coax the tractor either forward or backward over the ensuing thirty minutes of screaming tractor noises. Bill, meanwhile, the new law school graduate, sat on the bank, smoking a cigarette, and wondered about joining the Navy as a JAG officer and putting out to sea. Someplace far, far away from Barrington, Illinois.

Just before sunup, Arnie climbed down off his steed and confessed to Bill, "It won't budge."

"No shit, Sherlock," said Bill, "what was your first clue?"

Arnie almost answered, but by then he was far enough on the sober side of the new day that he realized Bill's question was purely rhetorical, if not sarcastic beyond all that was human and good.

"Eh, fuck off then," Arnie said to the tractor. "C'mon, let's go call Willard Rench."

Rench, remember, owned the Firestone Store and a huge dinosaur of a tow truck used to move eighteen-wheelers. Indeed, he'd be glad to run out and untangle Arnie's web before the sun was fully up and before the OOKK maintenance men came onto the scene as they did every day with their sprinklers, rakes, and hoes.

"Where are you, then?" asked Rench. "Did you say the Olde Orchard Kountry Klub?"

"That's right," Arnie said. "My tractor's stuck in a water hole."

"What the fug?" said Willard, always one to come right out and curse.

"That's right. I had an accident last night, Willard. I'd like you to come unscramble things before I'm caught out here."

"Do you honestly think I'd get mixed up in your crazies, Gresham? Do I look to you like I just fell off the turnip wagon?" Willard laughed before disconnecting.

"Thanks for nothing," Arnie said as he slammed down the phone.

"He's on the way," I take it, Bill said with another dose of sarcasm. "I'm going home."

"Hey," said Arnie as he watched Bill strike out across the golf course. "No thanks for giving you a ride home?"

Bill didn't answer. Head down and walking as fast as he knew how he was leaving the scene. That's what we call it now, we criminal lawyers. Leaving the scene. It's what all common criminals do after they've committed their crime.

But not Arnie. He backed away from the pond, sat down hard on the hillock sloping down to the pond, threw his head back, and bawled.

Cleveland, our father, managed to get the criminal case assigned to a close friend of his at the State's Attorney's Office where he used to work. The OOKK officers and board wanted someone to go to jail. They wanted restitution. And they wanted front-page fines. Fines big enough that the *Tribune* posted stories on page one.

So Cleveland did the next indicated thing. He let it all cool down.

Six months later, Arnie pled guilty to destruction of private property and paid a $2500 fine. There was also restitution of $35,000 to the OOKK.

My dad got his 1965 MGB green-over-black sports car back, fully rehabbed. It cost another three grand, which Arnie also paid.

Arnie now remembers that night fondly.

Bill Howerton, my old friend and Arnie's co-adventurer at the OOKK, is now a Captain in the United States Navy and has just received his second command, a destroyer deployed somewhere in the waters of the Middle East.

"Talk about a water hole," Arnie said of Bill one night when our family had just sat down for dinner around our vast oak table.

My father's head snapped up. "What was that?"

"Bill's overseas somewhere off Qatar."

"And that's what reminded you of the waterhole on seven?"

"Sorry, Dad. I didn't realize we were still touchy about that."

Dad chased a load of peas around his plate with a solid silver fork. "Nuts to you both," he muttered. "Nuts to you especially, Arnie. You always were a handful."

"Sorry, Dad."

My mom laughed first, followed by my dad. Arnie looked at me. I could only shrug. I'd never known parents could recover from their kids.

It was a good thing to know.

Chapter 25

MICHAEL

When I finally earned my law degree and passed the Illinois Bar Exam, I was twenty-four years old. It was 1985, almost 1986. After seven years of college, I was restless. There had to be more to life than college and law school and work without letup. So, after spending my first years in my father's law practice, I went down to the Chicago recruiter and signed up for the Army JAG Corps just as Operation Desert Shield in 1990 got going. The build-up following led to Operation Desert Storm, a war waged by coalition forces from 35 nations led by the United States against Iraq in response to Iraq's invasion of Kuwait.

Following my six weeks at Army DCC in Georgia and JAG school in Virginia, Martha came to visit me in my office at Gresham Law Offices. I was in the process of taking an inventory of all open files just to be sure, for the third time, I had arranged for other attorneys to take them over.

When Martha arrived, the air conditioner in my office was beating out a steady marching rhythm from its window encasement. It was too hot to be outside, and inside, even in the AC, wasn't that much better. So I was moving slowly that day, struggling to keep awake after a substantial lunch of prime rib and mashed potatoes and gravy. Usually, I ate light or nothing at all for lunch so I could spend my hour running at the Downtown Athletic Club. The track was enclosed on the second floor of the building and was air-conditioned, so thirty minutes of work didn't bring you to your knees as the out-of-doors would have. But that day was one of resistance: I decided I preferred eating massive calories to running. I had a feeling that once deployed in Iraq, there would be plenty of time for runs.

Martha didn't have an appointment. She just showed up in my office. Mrs. Lingscheit, a recently married nineteen-year-old with superior secretarial skills buzzed me from the outer office. Would I see a Martha Bautista? Of course, I said. Martha was led right into my sanctum where we hugged, and I held her a few extra seconds. She was my grandfather's ancient housekeeper from long ago. We sat down, and she brought me up to speed.

She had married at long last and given birth to two children, a boy, and a girl. Her husband was a maintenance worker with the City of Schaumburg where they still lived; both retired now. I knew about her history in the war and how she had survived the hell of Japanese imprisonment. It amazed me enough, not to mention that she'd returned to the States and enjoyed a pretty normal life. Another interesting tidbit: Martha and Howie, her husband, always seemed to be included whenever Roland or Cincy threw a party or our clan attended a family function with my grandfather Knowles, now retired from the U.S. Senate and working on his memoirs. Yes, Martha and Howie were always around, so much so that I guess we all considered them part of the family. In fact, I called her Aunt Martha and always had. Howie wasn't Uncle Howie; he was just Howie.

So my Aunt Martha took a seat across from me at my desk and laid her cane across her legs. She was wearing a flowery print dress that looked to me like it was too heavy for the weather, but what did I really know about such things? Her hair was pulled back in a bun, and her bangs reached almost to her eyebrows. Her brown eyes all but matched the hair on her head which, after its weekly bottle trick, was itself still a rusty brown. Good for you, Aunt Martha, I remember thinking. The hell with gray hair. Keep it brown if that's what you want. Hell, dye it blond if you like; you certainly have earned the right.

"So what's up, Aunt Martha?" I began. "And where's Howie?"

"He dropped me in front and went to park the car. He'll be here."

I waited. She would connect it up if I were patient.

She began, "I've needed to talk to someone about this, Michael. You remember the Nine Fingers case, of course."

The killer of a dormitory full of student nurses—who didn't remember? "Of course. The murderer that wanted to cross you off his list one night."

"Yes, but he couldn't find me."

"Thank God. So what about him? It still bothers you, I expect."

"Bothers me? I still don't sleep well, Michael. That's why I'm here."

"How can I help?"

"You can find Nine Fingers. If you can find him and kill him, then maybe I can get a full night's sleep again before I die. That is my one remaining hope, that I get to enjoy a peaceful night's sleep before I pass."

Just like that—kill someone for me, please, like ordering a burger with fries.

"Hadn't thought about killing anyone, Aunt Martha."

"I have no one else to turn to, Michael. And you, of all people—a man of the law—knows he has it coming."

"Uh—how do I find this guy? I'm not saying I'll kill him for you. I'm just wondering how I'd find him if I decided to do it."

She seized her cane and pointed the rubber end at me. "You're the lawyer, Michael! You tell me, son."

So that was it. She was going to send me off to find a guy who had been missing, what, twenty-five years now? A guy no one could confirm was even alive? I felt bewildered by her request. But on the other hand, you didn't refuse Aunt Martha. She was family.

"How about I do what I can and, if I hit pay dirt, I have him arrested? Would that work for you, Aunt Martha?"

"It wasn't what I had in mind. He deserves to die, Michael. He doesn't deserve a trial. He didn't give all those nurses a trial."

So I accepted...conditionally. "All right, Aunt Martha. I'll find him for you. I'll never stop looking, either. I promise you that. But I won't kill him. I'll only see that he goes to prison."

Tears glossed her eyes. "Don't let me down with nice words about justice, Michael. Kill this snake for me and for all the girls he murdered for absolutely no reason on God's green earth!"

I was about to make another comment about doing justice as a lawyer versus murdering someone without due process, but the door opened behind her.

Howie came lurching into my office, out of breath and hand extended to shake. I went to grasp his hand, but he walked right past and enveloped me in a bear hug. "Mikey, good to see you, boy. You should come see me sometime. We'll share a cold one and watch the Sox."

"All right, Howie. I'll make a point of doing that. But first, you guys, I need to tell you that I'm being deployed to Iraq in the next little while."

"Going to kick Saddam's ass?" Howie asked.

"Something like that." I sat down again and motioned for Howie to take the seat next to Aunt Martha. "No, actually, nothing so exciting. I'm a lawyer in the army, so I expect they'll have me doing courts martial for troops caught drinking and driving on base. Important stuff like that."

"Doesn't matter, Michael," said Aunt Martha. "We're just proud of you for serving."

I whispered conspiratorially, "I'm just doing it so I can wear a uniform and maybe catch a wife."

Martha and Howie exploded laughing. "Oh sure," Howie said, "you need a uniform for that."

"Howie, Michael has agreed to kill Nine Fingers for me. Isn't he wonderful?"

"Whoa, Aunt Martha. I've agreed to try and find him. What happens after that will probably be a trial. Maybe the state will put him to death. But I don't think killing him is something a lawyer is allowed to do."

Her eyes narrowed and fixed on my eyes. "Do not mock me, Michael."

"I'm sorry. Yes, I'll try to find him. No, I probably won't kill him."

"Then you will disappoint me, Michael."

"It's the best I can do. Tell you what, let me hunt him down and report back to you. He's probably dead by now anyway, with his record of violence, so our discussion is moot. Let's go a step at a time."

"That makes sense," said Aunt Martha. "That makes good sense."

We then branched off into other conversations: family, baseball, the weather, and Grandfather's memoirs, which I think caused Aunt Martha to suddenly feel uncomfortable. I didn't pick up on her discomfort at the time until things connected in my mind much later, so I just kept up a dialogue with them until it was clear we'd run out of things to talk about. They went home and left me sitting there, wondering what I actually would do if I were on the business end of a gun trained on a mass murderer. Probably take him to the cops. I had no history of violence in me except getting beat up one day in the boys' restroom in fourth grade because I had raised my hand too much when the teacher asked the class questions. That was about it.

But then something happened to change my mind. The day before I was to fly to Iraq, the *St. Louis Post-Dispatch* ran a story about a family of four murdered near Greenville, Illinois, a town about forty miles east of St. Louis. This wouldn't ordinarily turn my head, except this time there was a survivor, a ten-year-old girl left for dead, who described the man's left hand. Four fingers, missing ring finger.

Then I knew. He was still out there.

I committed at that moment. I was going to take the hunt very seriously when I returned from Iraq.

And, given the opportunity, I was going to shoot the son of a bitch myself.

Chapter 26

MICHAEL

I did get to Kuwait, but not to Iraq, in 1991. The so-called war lasted only a few weeks for me. And I never fired a single shot. Then it was over. I was deployed to the Middle East all of six months, living and working at an enormous base in Kuwait. My assignment was pretty much as I'd told Aunt Martha and Howie, prosecuting minor violations of the Army's criminal code. DWI's, AWOL's, fights—these kept me busy while "in-country." My combat was inside air-conditioned courtrooms where fresh water was set out in pitchers on counsel table twice a day, and clean bedsheets were the norm. Still, outside of our base, the country was in the Stone Age. There wasn't enough water for the population, no crops could be grown thanks to the climate, and sandstorms kept everything covered in grit year-round. It wasn't a beautiful place.

I returned to Iraq a second time as an Army reservist in 2004 after our forces had taken Baghdad and were fighting the Saddam loyalists who had turned to car bombs and IEDs as their preferred weapons of choice. This second visit was much different from my first visit in the early 90's and was almost civilized. Our plane touched down in Kuwait. Then we were trucked into Iraq, to the Green Zone, a supposedly safe area for America and its allies smack dab in the center of Baghdad. Our old troop transport rumbled through the gates, and I remembered, coming off the bus, this much about Iraq: the heat made a Chicago summer seem cool by comparison. I looked out over the desert and could see the heat rising in shimmering layers from the sand. Luckily, though, my quarters were air-conditioned, a huge relief. So was the Justice Building where I was assigned to work. Maybe it wasn't going to be so bad.

I was not a deep thinker back then, not that I ever have been. I navigated my days by reacting to new situations. It would be years before I learned to be proactive; back then, I was but a bystander, an observer, almost, to my own life.

Afternoons, after court finished for the day, I most always ambled over to the Army Club for a scotch. I was lonely in Iraq with none of the brotherhood that I'd heard existed among the grunts, the soldiers who had each other's backs all day. It was said they loved their army brothers and they'd die for one another. Nothing like that existed in my life. Hell, I had trouble scrounging up a drinking buddy most afternoons. But lawyers are like that in war zones, standoffish and secretive since many of them were putting soldiers behind bars—not a way to win a popularity contest with the most heavily armed men the world had ever seen.

After court had shut down one day in July, I stopped by the Army Club, not to drink but to find the lawyer who was defending a female sergeant I was prosecuting. He wasn't in the Army Club after all, so I turned to leave. Just as I was heading out, a soldier arose from a table next to the entrance and blocked my path. He was heavily muscled, with thick black hair cut military short. He looked to be the kind of guy you see in the Army every once in a while, the guy nobody wants to mess with. The type of guy everyone knew might one day shoot his commanding officer in the back of the head if he was foolishly exposing his men to a situation no one should walk into. That kind of guy.

Anyway, he stood up and blocked me and motioned that I should sit at his table. So, I did.

His name was Marcel Rainford. Marcel was serving his second of two tours as General Dumont's driver—meaning he was a bodyguard who didn't get to shoot anyone because he was guarding a four-star Army general and escorting him around Baghdad in an Army Humvee. General Dumont, as it happened, was the commander of all JAG forces in Iraq, which made him my commander and meant it was very common to bump into him in the Justice complex where I spent my days.

Marcel was from "Europe" was all he would tell me. He had migrated to the U.S. and joined the Army after 9/11. There was a promise of U.S. citizenship after he finished his enlistment.

He was a swarthy, burly man with powerful shoulders and chiseled face. He reminded me of the guy you'd want on an Army recruiting poster, pointing his finger at you, saying, *Uncle Sam Wants You!*

That day, when he blocked me from leaving the Army Club, I did join him at his table as he requested.

We sat, and he ordered two beers. It went unsaid; I was having a beer too, although I seldom drank beer. Scotch was my poison of choice back then. I shrugged and accepted the mug when it arrived. We each took a long swallow, and he wiped his mouth with the back of his hand. No wedding ring, I saw.

"I've seen you around the Court Complex," he said matter-of-factly.

"I've seen you, too," I said, thinking this was probably going to lead somewhere.

"You're a lawyer," he added.

"Yes, I've had a license about five years now."

"Where you from? Let me guess, Minneapolis?"

"Not too far off. Chicago, actually."

"The Windy City."

"Born and raised. My dad's a lawyer. My grandfather was a cop and a politician."

"That's what I did before—I was a cop. Well, sort of a cop."

"What does 'sort of a cop' mean, exactly?"

"I worked for Interpol."

"Tracking down bad guys?"

"Yes. And before that, I was at Scotland Yard. That's where I broke in."

"So tell me, Marcel, have you caught some bad guys at Interpol?'

"I have. Some terrible guys."

"Anyone I've heard about?"

"I located Carlos the Jackal in '94. I was there with the French agents in Khartoum when they took him down."

"No way!"

"Yes, way. On the flight from Sudan to Paris, we talked back and forth. He shared some stories with us. Now he's doing life."

"That is amazing. How did you find him?"

At that point, Marcel smiled and touched a finger to the side of his head. "Confidential, Captain. Sorry."

"Sure."

"So, what are you doing when you get out?"

"I don't know. Back to Chicago. Gotta make a living so I'll be doing law again. Unless something more exciting comes along."

"What kind of law?"

"Criminal. Defense."

"But over here you're prosecuting. You work both sides of the street?"

"Marcel, there's really only one side. And the street's name is 'Justice.'"

"You're one of those guys who still believe in the law, then?"

"What?" I asked in mock horror. "You don't?"

"A little of this, a little of that. It always depends."

"Depends on what?"

He smiled for the first time. "It all depends on who's paying me. Sometimes I follow the law; sometimes I am the law. We're different, kiddo, you and me."

"Maybe not so different. Let me ask you something. My Aunt Martha survived a mass murder. Some effing barge deckhand murdered a bunch of nurses Aunt Martha was living with. Now she wants me to find this guy and kill him."

"I can understand that. I'd feel the same way. How about you, Ace?"

"I won't know until I find him."

"Find him? That shouldn't be so hard. If you know how to look."

I moved closer to the table. "How would you look?"

"If it was me? I'd figure out where he works and wait outside the factory."

"He must have worked on river barges. That's all we can figure."

"That makes it even easier. Get a card and start working barges."

"What kind of card?"

"Union card, Michael. My God, man. You're never going to find the guy."

"I have an idea. What if I hire you to find him for me?"

"Could be, could be. How much are you paying?"

"Never done this before," I said. "How about I pay you five grand if you bring him to me?"

"No, how about you pay me ten grand, and I take you to him? You can figure out what to do from there. Fair enough?"

I reached across the table, my hand outstretched. He reached across, and we shook hands.

"When you out?" he asked.

"Six months. You?"

"Same. See you back in Chicago." He downed his beer, swiped his hand across his mouth, and stood to leave.

"Wait. Don't you want my address or phone or something?"

"Captain Gresham, you leave a trail ten feet wide. I won't be needing your number. One day I'll show up at your front door. Or use your attorney wiles and find me. I'll have your killer inside thirty days. Thirty days or you pay me nothing."

"Fair enough, then."

He squared his shoulders and headed outside into the unforgiving desert sun.

I stayed behind and quietly finished my beer.

Six months and one week later, I saw Marcel again.

Chapter 27

MICHAEL

When I returned to Chicago, I found an office because it was time step out on my own. The building was the Monadnock Building, just around the corner from the federal courts. The office consisted of four quite small private offices, a waiting room with a receptionist cut-out, a spotless and well-kept bathroom, a supplies/printer room, a tiny kitchen with microwave and refrigerator, and skylights throughout.

As I said, the federal courts were nearby. My goal was to become proficient in those courts since I'd already spent five years in the state courts. In this way, I'd become a criminal defense lawyer who was comfortable in any court in downtown Chicago. It was a good plan, and my father approved. I could tell, when I told him, that he'd been holding out a bit of hope that I'd rejoin his firm when I returned from overseas. But he didn't let it show. Far from it. Cleveland Gresham was his own man, and he had raised me to be the same way: to make my own decisions and not force myself on others but to observe loyalty to family above all else, even the law. That's just how it was.

One of my first stops on my return was to visit my Aunt Martha. My ulterior motive in visiting her was to see if she'd agree with me helping put Nine Fingers in jail instead of murdering him outright. I was still holding onto the hope that justice done in the courts was just the same to her as justice done at the end of a nine-millimeter. But I didn't know.

Aunt Martha and Howie lived in Schaumburg on the street named, of all things, Braintree Road. When I was much younger, the name always made me think of human brains scattered through the branches of some tree. Maybe I wasn't too far wrong considering Aunt Martha's request now that I was grown. In fact, near as I could tell, brains scattered anywhere would suit her just fine, as long as they belonged to Nine Fingers.

So I knocked on the storm door and waited. Before long, the inside door was unlocked, and then a hand came out and unlocked the storm door. I could see how Aunt Martha was living, with locks and shutters, and in one way I didn't blame her.

Howie invited me inside. He sat me down in the living room and offered coffee. It was March and freezing outside, and coffee sounded just about right. Minutes later, he returned with a mug of brew. I chided Howie how he was all Navy and had never gotten over the mug thing.

Before long, Aunt Martha, wearing a blue robe, buttoned neck to knee, glided into the room, bent over the back of my chair, and gave me a bear hug. "I'm so glad you're home safe and sound," she whispered to me. "My favorite grandson."

I thought it odd she would refer to me as a grandson, but I naturally let it go. She was old, and she could refer to me however she liked. The prerogative of advancing years and all that.

She sat across from me in a dull yellow wingback chair. The arms featured doilies that, I was all but certain, she had crocheted herself. In fact, looking around, all seating featured doilies. Now I knew what she did in her spare time. So I thought, at least.

"Wait one," she promptly said and jumped up—spry, yes—and left the room. Minutes later, she returned, carrying what looked to be a scrapbook.

She knelt down beside me, placed the book on my lap, and told me to start paging through. I complied and was greeted by page after page of newspaper accounts of mystery murders all across the U.S. The stories spanned the last dozen or so years, and the cases happened as far away as Maine and Seattle. I was dumbfounded. Then the light went off in my head. She was looking for patterns, looking for clues as to where Nine Fingers might strike next, if any of these crimes were the work of Nine Fingers at all, of course.

"Well?" she asked when I closed the back cover.

"Impressive, Aunt Martha. But what does it tell you?"

She laughed and squeezed my shoulder as she crept back to her chair. "It tells me it ain't hardly safe to go outside anymore, Michael."

We laughed. Howie came into the room, carrying a cup of coffee upon a saucer for his wife.

She took a sip and nodded at him. "See? No mugs for Aunt Martha. Cups and saucers, the civilized way."

We laughed again, and I figured that was as good a time as any to broach the subject of just how I would dispose of Nine Fingers. If I even found him.

"Aunt Martha, we saw a lot of killing in Iraq," I began.

She cleared her throat. "World War II in the Philippines was worse, I'm guessing," she reminded me with a look that said she already knew where I was going with this.

"Well, killing is killing regardless of quantity," I suppose. "Anyway, I'm thinking about this Nine Fingers guy. I think the greater punishment for him would be to have to live out his life behind bars. It would make him think about the people he killed, every minute of every day. I'm guessing it would drive him mad, and he might even hang himself."

"Nicely played, Michael," she said with a slight smile and a nod of the head, "but no cigar. I want the man dead, period. You promised me, Michael."

Well, that wasn't entirely true, but I suppose it's what she thought she'd heard. At that moment I wished my mother was there with me to try to talk some sense into Aunt Martha. My mother excelled at slow, steady, logical discussion when faced with a problem. I was sure she could convince Aunt Martha to see things my way.

It was the first time in my life I'd faced a situation where my parents' rules for me—thou shalt not kill—were in serious conflict with the wishes of a client. Well, almost a client. But it wouldn't be the last, and it wouldn't ever get any easier, learning to do what was required instead of what was right. They weren't always the same, not around the courtrooms where I worked. That isn't to say I didn't sometimes have to fire clients when they went off the rails. I did fire plenty, dozens of them, in fact. But my professional life always included ambiguity. Welcome to the practice of law.

I sat there beside myself. I didn't know what else to say or how to say it. So I tried a different approach. "Finding him is going to be extremely difficult," I said.

She smiled. "Not for a lawyer of your caliber. My guess is, you're hot on his trail already."

Sweet Jesus. This was going nowhere fast.

So I changed the subject altogether. "You going to catch any White Sox spring games?" I asked Howie.

Before Howie could answer, Aunt Martha was all over me. "Promise me you're not going to let me down, Michael. Find this son of a bitch and kill him. Squash him like a bug then scrape him off your shoe. Then, just maybe, your poor Aunt Martha can get a decent night's sleep for the first time in thirty years."

Howie looked helplessly in my direction. I could see he probably heard about Nine Fingers and Aunt Martha's thirst for blood much more often than I. My heart went out to him just a little.

So, with nowhere left to turn, no place left to hide, I said what I'd gone there to say. "I'm going to find him, Aunt Martha. Whether I kill him or the state kills him or some inmate shivs him, that's to be decided. I'm not making any promises either way."

"You already promised. Don't go back on it, Michael."

"This time I might have to, Aunt Martha."

When I said that, she abruptly stood, knocking the coffee cup and saucer from her knee and spilling the liquid across the carpet. She lifted her chin up high and stalked from the room. "A promise is a promise," she tossed back over her shoulder. "Gresham men always keep their word. Look it up, Michael."

I was finished there. I snuck out the front door while Howie scurried off in search of cleaning supplies.

Driving away, I now knew one thing. I was going to need help. Lots of help.

I couldn't wait any longer for Marcel to find me. It was time for me to call my old buddy.

Marcel would know what to do and how to do it.

It wouldn't be the last time a call to Marcel would be necessary.

Chapter 28

MICHAEL

Marcel came to America after a contract was issued on his life by a group of angry Sicilian Mafiosi. They were mad that he'd interrupted the flow of heroin into Europe from Turkey. Word of the contract on his life got back to his captain at Interpol, and he sent two agents to sidetrack the three killers Sicily had sent after Marcel. At the same time, Interpol swapped with the U.S. State Department. Marcel was sent to the U.S. under an entirely new identity. He became just another number in the State's terabytes of bureaucracy. After less than one year of working undercover for the U.S. Marshal's Service, Marcel was shot in the face and received medical retirement. He told his friends at the USMS so long and moved far away to Chicago. Around that time, 9/11 saw the buildings come down in New York, and shortly after that, Marcel enlisted in the U.S. Army. Off to Iraq he went, ready to serve his adopted country.

Rather than assigning Marcel to the killing of Iraqis, however, he wound up in Iraq working as a bodyguard for the head of the Judge Advocate General. Marcel was his driver, drinking buddy, and confidante. He lost quite a bit of faith in any future he might have in the military, so after completing his enlistment, Marcel returned to Chicago where he joined up with me. I was a JAG officer who'd caught the general's attention because I never lost at trial. I was sending everyone to the brig regardless of rank and bluster. When Marcel encountered me that late afternoon in the Army Club, we became best friends. He hasn't let me down since. Not even come close.

Nine Fingers' days were about to come to an end.

Chapter 29

MICHAEL

When Marcel and I said our goodbyes in Baghdad, we knew we'd meet again in Chicago. The year was 2007. After all, he'd had me agree to pay him ten grand if he came to my office and produced Nine Fingers in thirty days. Well, it hadn't quite worked out that way, despite Aunt Martha's demands. I hated to say I had other work more pressing than Nine Fingers but I did.

My criminal practice was bustling, and the reason for my success was simple: I worked at uncovering all the facts of all cases until I had the facts on my side. If the facts wouldn't turn around to be on my side, then I did what all criminal lawyers do—I hired an expert witness to explain to my juries why things were not as they seemed. I was improving every day in learning to sell to juries my alternate views of the universe, my alternative pictures of reality. Juries, I was learning, need a reason to turn someone loose when they were guilty but justice demands otherwise.

For example, I watched a broken father leap over the courtroom railing in a criminal trial I was following. He jumped the defendant from behind and snapped his neck. Why? Because the guy had molested then murdered the man's daughter. As it turned out, I was later hired to defend that father. This was one of those cases where he was guilty of the crime charged—homicide—but where the jury wanted to set him free. So I hired an expert to come to court and explain why the father lost control and killed someone. You would too, he told the jury, if it had been your child. Hell, the jury ended up thinking my client, the father, had done the city a service and turned him loose after only forty-five minutes of deliberation. Not guilty, they said. The story hit the media, and my client load suddenly doubled again. "Michael Gresham's Alternate Reality" was the title of a *Tribune* article in September of 2008. I hired two lawyers to help me cover court calls and motion practice. Busy, busy, busy.

So that was the scene Marcel walked into when he answered my call, surfaced in Chicago, and knocked on my door. I went over the situation with him. We talked about how we would work together, payment, and his freedom to investigate my cases without restraint from me. I quickly agreed with everything he wanted and needed. He started work the next morning. I couldn't have been happier, and I thanked the Lord every day for sending me Marcel.

One day, Aunt Martha cornered Marcel as he was leaving my office and she was coming in. She was older than Moses and as mobile and mentally sharp as ever. She used a walker and sometimes had difficulty with the *New York Times* crossword puzzle, but who didn't? She knew who Marcel was; she also knew he was her passkey to finding Nine Fingers. She needed a word. So Marcel backtracked, brought her into my office, and requested a sit-down with her right then and there. I agreed, of course, outnumbered as I was.

I helped her into her chair and set her walker aside. She wasted no time in telling Marcel what she wanted. "Michael has agreed to find the man for me, for which I am grateful. I'm certain he brought you onboard to help him do just that and keep his promise to his dear aunt."

I could feel Marcel's eyes on me; I didn't blink.

"Excuse me, Aunt Martha," Marcel said as he sat, "but what do we know about this man?"

Aunt Martha reached into the enormous handbag hanging from her walker and withdrew three thick folders.

"Lucky for us, I have the police reports right here. The crime scene reports, all that mess, you can review at the police station. But these are the officers' statements. You can look them over and see what we know about the man."

Marcel accepted the folders from her and said, "Well, can you just give me a quick summary so we can discuss today?"

"We know he was an itinerant deckhand."

"We know that how?"

"The police canvassed the entire Loop. No hotel, no boarding house, no flophouse, no motel had registered such a man two weeks before the tragedy and two weeks after. They talked to everyone. So they say he was itinerant. Their words, not mine."

"What does he look like?"

"That one's mine. I told them he was maybe average height. I made that estimate by how tall he was compared to the bunk beds."

"Color? Black man? White man? What?"

"White man. I never did see his face. Remember, I was hiding under the bed."

"But Michael tells me you saw his left hand."

"I did. Four fingers. No ring finger."

"Anything else about that hand?"

"No. But there was something else. Only the police know this."

"What's that, Aunt Martha?"

"He was whistling."

"Any song?"

"*That Old Black Magic.*"

"That's a street name for heroin," Marcel said to me. "Black Magic heroin. Comes from Turkey by way of Panama."

"Amazing," I said. His grasp of such things was reassuring, even more so the longer I knew the man. "So our man was either randomly whistling an out-of-date tune from long ago, or he was whistling irony. Ironic in the fact that the black magic of the song could have been referencing the black magic heroin pulsing through his veins as he went from girl to girl slicing throats."

"I'm guessing it's the latter," Marcel said. "He knew what the hell he was whistling."

We looked at Aunt Martha. She nodded. "Agree. He knew."

"Well, then," I said, "don't we need more time in Panama, Marcel?"

"Panama City. That's my jumping-off point."

"What happens there?" I asked.

He pursed his lips, thinking. Then, "I hire onto a tugboat. Learn my way around. Start the search from the deck of a tug this time."

Part IV

MARCEL

Chapter 30

MARCEL

My name is Marcel Rainford and my boss, Michael Gresham, tells me I'm an enigma. We'll see about that.

I killed my first man over a blood dispute. The wrong blood was running in the veins of the man having his way with my mum—because it wasn't my pop's blood. My pops was a lorry driver and always at the other end of England, which is when the pumper came calling on my mum. He'd run me outside and lower all the shades and lock all the doors. Thirty minutes later he'd emerge on the front porch, stretch his arms like he owned the place, belch, and pull his suspenders up over his shoulders. He'd hock and spit to the ground then light a fag. Just then, our eyes would meet, and he would do the absolute worst thing with me he could—he'd give me a wink. Which meant I was in on him jamming up my mum while my pops was off busting ass to bring home the goodies. That wink was one step too far.

So when my pop caught his ride on a southbound lorry that Sunday night in October, All Hallow's Eve, I hadn't finished cleaning my single-shot .20-gauge shotgun. Which explained why my gun didn't go into dad's lockup with the other guns before he caught his ride. Which had always been the rule: No Dad, No Gun. But he didn't give it much notice that night at all, me still at the rag and oil and elbow grease. No, he just hugged my mum, gave off with a pretend chop to my neck, tousled my hair, and looked disparagingly at my gun. But he didn't say anything except maybe that he trusted me enough with the gun to put it away even with him gone and all. Which was my intent.

But when the door closed behind my pops, I knew. I knew what I had to do. Sunday nights it was my mum's habit to traipse off down the hall to the bathroom and wash and dry her hair. With the bathroom door closed, it gave me the time I needed to stow my shotgun in its soft case, snuggle a box of .20 gauge shells along the stock, and zipper up things nicely. Then I crept out the front door, out into the chill, moonless night. My pops had left the porch light burning, but my mum always allowed fifteen minutes to pass and then she'd get up from the telly and switch off the light. So when I crept out like a bandit cradling a baby—my shotgun—it was pure, pitch black. You couldn't see the limelight up a green frog's arse. Out to the barn, slip inside, lean the shotgun case against the inside corner and hurry back inside the house. No one saw me; I saw no one. But I knew he would come. If not tonight, then tomorrow. And I knew I'd be ready for that wink next time. His final wink.

Monday I stayed home. A sore throat left me with such a hoarse voice I couldn't recite at school. I was fourteen and when we began that school term, I quickly learned that each student would recite every day. "Too hoarse, Mum," I signed and gurgled. "Staying home."

"You'll not," she shot back at me. Angry, though I didn't know why. What was it to her? She had no job to service, no housework—not to speak of—no dying relative to tend, so what difference could it make that I stayed at home with my illness? Such was the innocence of the child, yes?

"You'll clean out the barn today," she said in her official voice. "Starting at midday."

"Why noon?"

"You can laze around in bed until then. Maybe you are and maybe you aren't skiving. I don't know. But in case you do have the sore throat, you'll be over it by noon. Fourteen-year-olds are always well by noon on a school day. Don't forget, my lamb, I was once fourteen myself. I know how it goes."

I would've whined some, but in our part of Yorkshire you didn't dare complain one minute and lie to the police the next. Lie to the police? Maybe that's what was coming.

While I counted dust motes over my bed, my mum disappeared into the bath, and I could hear the water pipes moan and squeal. She'd spend a good ten minutes, all told, getting herself lovely. For just a flicker of a second, I almost thought she was making herself ready for him, but I slammed the door on that thought before it could become mine. She was loyal to my pops, and that was that. The other man was forcing himself on her; I was positive about that. My mums wouldn't hold sway with any man but pops. Hold onto that thought, I told myself, for all you're worth.

On my way outside, passing the bath, I heard the spigots squeal. The noisy flow of water ceased falling into the tub. So I snuck down the hall and around the corner, opened my dad's unlocked gun case, and nicked his pistol. I checked, and it was loaded. Then into my back pocket. At the front door, I snagged my coat off the peg, pulled my hat down low on my forehead, and stepped out onto the porch. I peered up at the sky. No sun. This time of year was always overcast. No sun meant no advantage to the shooter with the sun at his back. So far, we were even. I'd change that, however.

Sure enough, I'm not out in the barn twenty-minutes when I heard the sound of dusty automobile brakes squealing. I peeked out around the corner.

It was him. His name was Olivera Sanchez. I believed he was up from Spain, but that was the extent of my knowledge about the bollocks that shagged my mum.

Then he stepped inside my house without so much as a knock or hallo. I came away from my peek shaking my head. Nervy bastard, that one. I stopped all thought when I reached for the gun case. It wouldn't do to think too much from there on. So it became mechanical, my first time at a gunfight.

It was a good hour before the front door suddenly sprung open. He followed, stretching and belching like he just ate a ham. His eyes were down, following the flame as he lit his fag when I stepped out of the barn and trained my shotgun on his chest. He didn't notice until I got within twenty feet of him and he suddenly looked up and sidestepped once. But he saw the look on my face and knew better than to run. "Sonny," he said, "I din't know you was a' home!"

"I knew you would be coming," I said in a voice from my chest I'd never heard before. The voice of a man. "So I figured formal introductions was in order."

He smiled and flicked away his unfinished cigarette. He walked toward me, daring me to shoot before he could jerk the gun away and clock me in the head.

He took one step toward me and in the next second—a second that felt as long as sixty-seconds all strung out—I pulled the cold wooden gunstock to my cheek, kept both eyes open over the near end of the gunsight until I saw the BB at the other end of the barrel. I centered the BB just to the left of his heart—my left, not his—and, without hesitating I squeezed the trigger. "Blam!" The familiar roar and muzzle flash almost had me looking to the sky for a falling bird.

But I didn't look in that direction. I kept my eyes on Mr. Sanchez. It was like someone had taken a heavy ax and cut him open from shoulder to bottom rib. The lungs flew out the back, the heart was shredded, the eyes closed, and I was already after him, removing dad's pistol from my pocket and placing it inside the tightly wrapped fingers of his right hand. I knew he was right-handed—he smoked with his right and lit his fag with his right. Any fool would know that.

Then I pulled the trigger on that gun for him and shot myself in the fleshy part of my lower leg. I forced myself to stagger back across the grass to where I'd been standing when I fired. Then I went down, pulling my knee to my chest and calling for my mum.

Sometime later, the ambulance came and sped me off to hospital. They put me under and patched me up.

The next morning, a police inspector visited me in my room at the hospital. I was in a dingy gray room with six others. Only private health care got you a private room. "Shot you, did he?"

"That how it looks to you?" that same man's voice said from my mouth. I was lying in bed in a hospital gown, the cold sheets up to my waist.

"Yes, it does. You're lucky you didn't die." The officer sat in the plastic visitor chair to the left of my bed.

"Let's leave it there, then," I smirked. "Let's leave it at the thing you call luck."

"Who shot first?"

"He did. One shot. I shot on the way to the ground. Lucky shot, as we know."

"He shot you?"

"Yes."

"Then your luck held and you shot him?"

"That's right."

"Why did he shoot you?"

"I told him if he ever mounted my mum again I was going to kill him."

"Right. So you had the intent."

"I suppose I did."

"But he shot first?"

"Didn't we do that one already?"

The inspector leaned back in the plastic chair and gripped his knee with his hands. "Why on earth would he have your pa's gun?"

"You'll have to ask him that."

"Mr. Sanchez?"

"That's the one what had it. I'm sure he had a good reason. At least to him."

"And you had your shotgun why?"

"I'd been out in the woods trying to scare up our supper. Just returning home."

"Did you kill anything?"

I gave him the look that other men, like the inspector, wouldn't see coming either. "Only Mr. Sanchez. I killed him."

The nurse came in and dosed me good with pain pills, and I didn't see the inspector until four days later after I got home. He was waiting on the porch when my pops opened my passenger door and helped me out.

"This about where he was standing?" the inspector called to me.

"I don't know. The medicine's robbed me of any memory of the whole ordeal."

"You'll be no help then," the inspector called back, as much to my father as to me.

"I'm not your man," I said. "No memory."

"What about your mum? Did you spot her anywhere around that day?"

I limped toward the porch but didn't ascend the stairs. "She told me in the hospital she didn't know the man. She figured he broke in and nicked pa's gun. He meant to have his way with her."

"So you saved her as well as yourself."

"Your words, inspector. I don't recall."

"She told you this at the hospital?"

I could only give a slight nod since I grimaced in pain coming up the walk.

Suspicion painted the officer's face, but he nodded at both me and my pa as he walked down the steps and then left.

"That was close," I whispered to my pops.

"Go easy, son. It's done now."

A half-hour later they brought me tea and told me how happy they were I'd survived.

My dad lifted his cup in a toast.

"Here's to all the lies she never told me."

It was then I understood.

He knew it all.

And he was staying.

Chapter 31

MARCEL

After high school, it was three years to earn my law degree at York. I worked nights patrolling the grounds and buildings for campus security, catching four hours sleep before my first class the next morning. Then I was up all day for the coursework. It was a grind, but I was extremely motivated. I felt it was a matter of self-defense that I read the law in case the authorities ever decided to come after me for the murder of Olivera Sanchez. Thus far, they had applied the legal principle of self-defense, and I had escaped being charged with any crime. But in case Crown politics became such that my case got a second look, I wanted to be armed with the tools of a lawyer.

I met Aurelia in my second year of studies. She was a Level One; I was now a Level Two. We traded hellos in the law school lounge downstairs on the main floor. It consisted of five couches, eleven chairs, four study tables, and an old Irishman who ran a coffee and tarts cart in the corner. So I grabbed two pastries and two coffees and rejoined the Level One. It was October, chill in the air, warm woolens and rubber boots recommended. We sat in front of the fireplace and ate and drank our way into becoming friends.

Over time, I didn't have enough money to squire Aurelia around to the movies and plays and soccer matches as I would have. So we spent much of our time in her room or mine, necking and pretending to study while we watched each other with quick glances and smiles. She was beautiful, and I was in love for the first time. Then we went all the way at the end of our school year before she returned to London for the summer break.

My heart was shattering as I saw her off at the train, and it was making me mad to see her go like that. So I threw myself into my summer studies and, come the fall, I was nominated to and voted into the school's law journal. Law journal was always a tremendous honor and was based entirely on your grades. I ranked third in my class as a Level Three, so I was a shoo-in.

Aurelia had written me that her train would arrive in York on August 20. So there was I, down at the station, a bouquet in one hand and a box of chocolates in the other. The train finally pulled in nearly an hour behind schedule. My heart was pounding as the flood of passengers parted on either side of me. I knew that I would spot her blond hair and sparkling blue eyes at any moment and I was so, so in love, I could have burst.

But the passenger flow slowed to a trickle, and then there was nothing. It seemed they had all passed me by.

So I climbed onto the train and went from car to car, thinking maybe she needed help with her bags or some such.

But there wasn't a soul on board besides the cleaning crew and me.

Down to the station, I trotted and up to the ticket window.

"Was Aurelia Gladstone on the train?" I asked.

The woman behind the bars looked at a list she kept clamped to a clipboard. "No, no Aurelia anybody. And no Gladstones."

"Please, look again."

She shrugged and did what I had begged for. This time her review was much faster. "Still no Aurelias and no Gladstones, sir."

My heart fell. I went back outside and sat on one of the benches alongside the tracks. I checked my watch. Just after noon. So I waited, thinking she'd be on the two o'clock. When it pulled in, I repeated the same feelings and sense of desperation as before. But to no avail. Still no Aurelia.

So I sat back down and waited for the four-thirty—the last train of the day.

Again, there was no payoff. She wasn't coming that day, it was clear.

Back to my room I ran and down the hall to the telephone.

A man answered on the third ring.

"My name is Marcel Rainford. I was supposed to meet Aurelia at the train in York today. Did she miss the train?"

I could hear a man's voice and a sudden intake of air. Then a sob. "Oh, Marcel! Aurie's gone! She's been murdered."

Stunned, I pulled the phone away from my ear. "That—that can't be," I stuttered. "We were going to study together this year and then I—"

"Sorry lad. Got to go. We're off to Bible study."

"Wait, when did this happen?"

"A week ago."

"But no one let me know."

"Aurelia played it very private. We knew you were probably out there somewhere, but we had no name, no number. I'm off now. What was your name did you say?"

"Marcel Rainford."

"Well, Marcel, I would suggest you seek your comfort in the Lord. Down on your knees and claim his healing for your life, lad."

The line then went dead. Just then, I had never felt so alone in my life.

But instead of giving into my feelings, I started thinking. All the tears and prayers in the world weren't going to bring back my beautiful lover. It was over and done, and I had to move on. With one exception. Someone had murdered Aurelia, that's what the man said. This much I knew—whoever had done this to my precious friend was going to have to pay. Was going to have to pay the ultimate price.

Working for security and the campus police, I had learned a few things, knew a few tricks. I even had a uniform, such as it was, with a police badge. They had me wear it when I directed traffic at the soccer matches on campus. Made me feel like a real copper, too.

In the next ten minutes, I watched, as if in a dream, as I dressed in that uniform, slipped the sap into my back pocket, and headed back to the train station.

There was an eight o'clock train to London. I passed the same lady a tenner and waited to board. In my job at the campus police, I'd had occasion to ring up the London police and exchange this information or that. I knew where they were, and I knew how to speak with them, one copper to another. So when I arrived in London later that night, it took but three phone calls before I found the jail holding the man arrested for the sexual assault and murder of Aurelia Gladstone. I grabbed a taxi and rode from the depot to the jail; it took all of twenty minutes in the light, Sunday night traffic.

Upon entering the station, I found the desk sergeant was a suspicious man. He studied me from top to bottom, wearing my uniform and such as that.

"Yes, constable," he finally greeted me, and I knew I'd passed his test.

"I'm here to interview the arsehole who murdered one Aurelia Gladstone. I understand he's in your lockup."

"Oh, that one. A real prat, that one."

"Sure, but I need to have a word. Can you take me to him?"

Without answering, he spoke into the public address, and soon a jailer in a blue suit and black oxfords walked over.

"Take the constable to have a word with Eben Naville."

"That one? Are you sure? He refuses to speak with anyone, sergeant."

"Nevertheless."

The man shrugged and led me to a long hallway, and we began our little excursion together. Locked doors were buzzed open at three stops until at last, we arrived at a cellblock where inmates were housed in single cells.

"Single-celled, is he?" I asked.

"All he wants to do is hit someone, so we locked him away back here."

"This is what they call the 'stir'?"

"It is."

"Fair enough."

"Will it do to speak through the door?"

"Never. I need a one-on-one with this man who we suspect might have murdered one of our students up at York."

"Yes, I see." He then unlocked the door separating me from the man who'd sexually assaulted and murdered my lovely Aurelia Gladstone. It was going to go poorly for this wanker.

"By the way, mate," I said to my friendly jailer, "do you have a tape recorder I could borrow. This one's going to confess tonight, and I want it on tape."

"We do. Please wait right there." He closed the door to the cell behind me. I turned, and there sat the arsehole on his cot. He was holding his head between his hands and rocking forward and back, forward and back. I could hear low moans emanating deep from his throat that sounded like a man being garroted.

"Eben," I said, "I've come to have a word with you, lad."

He didn't look up. Just sat there, lost in his own world, forward and back, forward and back, moan, moan.

So I proceeded to do what I'd come there for. When I was finished, the left half of his head had been bashed in by my sap. I wiped the blood and the gore off the lead-filled leather just as my friendly jailer returned.

"Jesus, man!" he cried upon unlocking the door and stepping inside the cell. "Jesus, man, you've killed the wanker."

"I don't know if he's dead. He attacked me, had me down on the floor, but I got lucky with my sap."

"Oh, Jesus, lad, you're in the shite now."

Well, I was, yes and no. Yes, I had to attend the inquest and testify; no, because they turned me out. I was free. My story, full of holes, was accepted. Of course, it had more to do with Eben Naville than me. Eben, it seemed, had been under suspicion for two other murders, one of them a twelve-year-old girl. So the powers weren't all that unhappy to see him go.

I returned to the police station after the inquest and walked up to the same sergeant as before. "How does a fellow get on here?" I asked him.

"Work for the police? You want to work for the London police?"

"I do."

He handed me a packet of forms to fill out. I told him I'd be back. Down the street, I went to a small, quiet pub where I ordered a pint and squeezed into a tiny booth. Two hours later, I had my forms ready and returned them to the sergeant.

Six months later, I was wearing a real uniform and walking a beat, the newest police constable in the entire city.

One year later I was tagged for the firearms force and received my first Glock 17, the handgun we all carried. I rated as an expert on our first visit to the range and never scored below that rating during the five years I worked for the Central London Police. Dad had taught me well.

It was a great weapon then; it's still a great weapon now that I'm in Chicago, carrying my gun concealed, doing whatever chores Michael Gresham directs my way.

After the CLP, I went to work for London Metro, Scotland Yard, where I learned everything there was to know about criminal investigation. At the end of five years, I was sent to Paris to join Interpol. From there, I traveled around the world disposing of bad guys usually by arrest, though not always. There were many that no one wanted to be returned to their homeland. They only wanted them stopped from whatever it was they were doing. I learned every trick in the book about how to find these wankers and put their lights out. It was said, by my colleagues, there wasn't a man, or woman, on earth who was safe from me if I only got the word.

Probably that was true.

MICHAEL

Chapter 32

MICHAEL

Marcel began his search for the missing mass murderer from the deck of a tugboat in Panama, just as he'd promised Aunt Martha.

First, however, had come deckhand school. Marcel knew nothing about working aboard a tug. So he looked around for training. I was impressed with how thorough he approached his investigations already. But this one passed anything I'd seen yet. He found an advertisement from Allied Canal Ships, looking for deckhands to work the Panama Canal.

Marcel started with a course in Able Seafarer training at a San Diego school. In forty hours, the certification class covered watch-standing, occupational health precautions, deck equipment and machinery, cargo and stores handling, berthing, anchoring and other mooring systems, shipboard maintenance and repair, and marine environmental solutions. At the end of the training, Marcel began looking for a particular job in a particular location.

He went to the offices of Allied Canal Ships and made an application. His work history was all fictional, of course, keeping in mind that he wouldn't put himself in any position where other workers might be harmed.

In late August, he was invited to interview, and two weeks later, he found himself boarding *Fidelity Sounder*, a tugboat that spent its life pulling and pushing ships through the Panama Canal.

Marcel knew the Turkey heroin trade made its way to the U.S. via the Canal. That knowledge, coupled with the *Old Black Magic* tune which quite possibly was a reference to the Turkish black magic heroin that was swamping the U.S. back in the Sixties, Seventies, and Eighties, provided him a starting point. His starting point was very tenuous, however, and Marcel knew that. It was a very slim hope he held that there was a connection between Turkey, the tune, and the killer. If it were there and he found it, superb. If it were there and he didn't find it, time to keep looking. If it weren't there and never had been, he'd never know the difference. So he climbed aboard, and the tugboat cast off for the eastern seaboard.

Twenty-one days later, Marcel was a veteran seaman. He'd seen and done everything the original job posting had called for and much more. Ships had been pulled and pushed through the Panama Canal. An engine fire had been doused. Two crewmen were injured, and he'd helped administer first aid until medical help was reached. He stood watch at anytime day or night on a routine schedule and sometimes on an emergency basis when another seafarer was ill. He helped maintain the deck and machinery until he was bathed in sweat and black as a grease monkey from crewcut to waist. He'd moored and cast off—he had done it all by then. He was also a changed man in those three weeks. Twenty-five adipose pounds sloughed off. A deep, mahogany tan lit up his face and torso with a look of excellent health. He was prospering, as well, for able seamen are paid an excellent wage, and so there was that.

But had he seen any evidence at all of drug smuggling?

Absolutely none.

And it wasn't because he wasn't watching and inquiring. Marcel naturally had a way of insinuating an interrogation into just about any casual conversation; his talks with other crew provided fertile ground to do that. But then the others dried up, refusing to discuss such things with him. He later found out it was because they thought he was an undercover narcotics officer so often did he talk about drugs, availability, and commerce.

The blackout period forced him to revise how and how often he could bring up the touchy subject of narcotics, mainly because all crew was subject to on-the-spot no-notice urine sampling at any time day or night. Test positive, and your boat would moor and put you ashore at the first available opportunity. And that was without regard to whether you had money to make it home or even to eat. Nothing mattered to the company except expelling you from among its numbers. So talk of drugs was verboten for the most part. Marcel, however, always the undercover agent, knew all the ways the traffickers and users might be found out, and he followed those impressions he had of such people.

On one particular Saturday night, the *Fidelity Sounder* put in at Coastal Fuel Service. It was a service for the maritime trade for the collection of marine slop oils, bilge water, and used oil for treatment, proper disposal, and recycling into renewable fuels and lubricant base oils. The new environmental rules affected all boats and ships in the process of transiting the Panama Canal before their final port of destination. In other words, such stops weren't optional, but mandatory. While Coastal went about its cleanup of the tugboat, Marcel and the *Fidelity's* crew headed for the Yellow Lampe.

The Yellow Lampe was an ale and skin house down by the docks. Its clientele was by and large boat and ship crews laying over for whatever reason. Upon receiving a shore pass, crew upon crew found themselves at the Lampe, the first tavern up from the main road that paralleled the docks, Frontage Road.

There, at the Lampe, he made his first contact.

After purchasing two rounds of ale for his crew-mates, Marcel sat back in his chair and lit a cigarette. "So," he said, "I'm wondering if anyone knows a sailor missing a ring finger."

Several of the crew immediately shook their heads. "No," said three of the seven boat-mates gathered around.

One mate, however, looked narrowly at Marcel. He was an old bastard, straggly gray hair, a drinker's nose, bulbous and red, and gnarly hands with yellow-stained fingernails. He'd been around a while, Marcel could tell. "What's it to you if I do know one like that?"

A shiver shot down Marcel's back. Might this be something? "It's worth a lot to me. He's a long-lost relative."

"Oh, yeah, how does that work?"

"His ex-wife has news for him about their child. I said I would keep my eyes open for him."

The mate waved him off. "Oh, that. The man I know has no wife."

"Ex-wife, sir."

"Well, that might be. The one I'm thinking of is an engine seafarer on the *Signet Tourer*. She's a tug with similar poundage." Meaning similar in size to the *Fidelity Sounder*.

"My friend would pay money to know more."

"How much would that be?"

"She can go as high as one-hundred dollars."

"Oh, that. I don't know about that."

"Plus, I told her I'd contribute another hundred. Their child is very ill, and he's needed at her bedside."

The old mate sighed. He upended his metal mug and drained it off. Then he raised the mug to Marcel, indicating another round was in order. Marcel immediately placed the order and then turned sideways to the table and withdrew his money clip. Five one-hundred-dollar bills huddled together inside the clip. Perfect. He fished out two bills, turned, and placed them Benjamin-up on the table between himself and the Mate. "Two hundred, sir. I'm waiting."

"Name of Richard Dotty. Engine seafarer on the *Tourer*. She's four vessels astern the *Sounder* as we speak. But be careful, friend. This man carries a long, sharp blade, and he ain't afraid to use it. I've heard stories."

Marcel watched the man greedily slip his fingers beneath the two bills, fold them, and place them in the breast pocket of his blue work shirt.

"Stories? Such as?"

"Just that he's gutted a man or two before. He don't suffer fools, believe me."

"Well, then we're even. I don't suffer fools myself."

The men gathered around the table laughed, and the moment passed. Marcel knew better than to go there again or he would draw suspicion, his excuse being such a minor one.

But his heart was pounding as he guzzled the last of his ale and stood to leave. "Got my lady waiting at the hotel," he explained for his sudden departure. "Gents, it's been real."

"Same on you, Marce," called out Ellory, the young cook.

"Thanks for the duty pay, sailor," quipped the Mate. "I see two young fillies in my future." Then Marcel was off.

* * *

The *Tourer* would be putting in at any time. Marcel knew it could be one of a hundred places where it tied up, as well. How would he locate it and identify Richard Dotty? He wracked his mind. Then it occurred to him. He turned on his smartphone and browsed to the boat's name. He found Curtis Marine owned the boat out of Panama City. So he called the central office and made his way through the menu to the dispatch office. He punched in the number and waited.

At long last, a female voice answered. "Curtis Marine at your service. How can we help, mate?"

"I'm looking for the port of call for the *Signet Tourer*. My wife's brother is aboard, and he's needed at home. There's a private family emergency."

"Name of the crewman?"

It was the first test.

"Richard Dotty. D-o-t-t-y."

"We don't have—no, wait. Here we are."

"Port?"

"MEC Shipyards, Balboa. Service call."

"That'll do. Do you have an ETA?"

"Oh-seven-thirty."

Tomorrow morning. Marcel checked his watch. Two a.m. Plenty of time to make it to Balboa.

"Thanks so much, miss."

"Your name sir, for my log?"

"Emanuel Gaona. I'm calling from Miami."

"Thank you, Mr. Gaona. Goodbye, now."

"So long."

He hung up and browsed back to MEC on his iPhone. There, he read an advertising blurb about what kind of work was done at MEC. Evidently, in-service collisions were big. Marcel wondered if that was the reason for the *Tourer* putting in, and he kicked himself for not asking, for it would make a huge difference in how long Richard Dotty might be in the locale. MEC also did pier repairs, as well as cleaning and polishing by SCUBA.

Marcel called for a taxicab. Twenty minutes later, he was in the backseat of a green-and-white checkered cab, headed for the Balboa location of MEC. He had the driver pull through a fast food joint where he purchased two burgers and large black coffee. It was going to be a long night. He chomped on the burgers as they wended their way northeast.

The taxi dropped him at MEC's main gate. A sleepy-eyed guard wearing a brown uniform, pistol, and bandolier stepped out of the guard house, reviewed his ID and Inland Boatmen's Union card, then told him to proceed ahead.

The central office was locked. Marcel pushed the press-to-talk button and spoke his name into the louvers.

A tinny voice crackled back. "Business, Mr. Gaona?"

"I'm meeting a boat-mate here. *Signet Tourer* mate."

"She's not due in for four hours. Sorry, sir, we don't have accommodations for sleeping."

"Do you have just a waiting room? I require very little."

"We do have that. Please pull the handle at the buzz."

A buzz followed, and Marcel pulled then walked inside.

Inside, at the reception desk, he asked the matronly woman wearing a black dress and a string of pearls whether she had the crew manifest for the *Signet Tourer*. She replied that she did not. "Would you like me to get you a cup of just-made coffee, Mr. Gaona?"

"I would pay some serious bucks for a cup of just-made."

She tossed off a laugh as she exited stage-right. "No need. We take care of our boat crews best we can. Be right back."

Marcel had the choice of a sofa or one of three Naugahyde chairs. He chose the couch. It would make an excellent place to stretch out.

"I'm Missy," the pearl lady said when she returned. She passed Marcel a green mug of steaming coffee. "I didn't know what you take. Most sailors like it black, so there you are."

"Black is perfect." He blew across the mug.

"So who are we here to see?"

"Crew by the name of Richard Dotty, an old acquaintance of my wife's sister."

"Goodness. It must be important, this time of night and all."

"Yes, very. Sick child back in Miami. Very sick."

"Goodness. Let me call on the transceiver and see if I can locate him on the *Tourer*. Would that help?"

Marcel's smile evaporated. "I think not. Mr. Dotty would wonder what's up, and I want to break the news to him. It's not good."

"Certainly, certainly. Well, you can sit back here and relax. Plenty of magazines on the coffee table. If you like, you can also stretch out. Please remove the steel toes first."

She meant the steel-toed work boots required of all hands.

"Yes, ma'am. I might take you up on that."

"We have an old army blanket. Would you like to borrow that?"

"Ah, yes."

"And a pillow, as well, though I don't know how clean it is."

"It'll do, I'm sure. That would be great."

"All right. Give me two ticks, and I'll be back."

Sure enough, she returned with a scratch army blanket that smelled slightly of mothballs, plus a too-soft feather pillow. He thanked her and began removing his shoes. "Siri," he said into his iPhone. "Set the alarm for oh-five-thirty, please."

Siri didn't understand the format, so he repeated it.

"Alarm for five-thirty a.m."

It was done. Two swallows of the steaming coffee and Marcel stretched out. He was asleep in minutes.

* * *

Siri awoke him at precisely five-thirty. Marcel sat up, pulled on his shoes and laced them, and hurried to the counter. The same pearl lady was there, typing on her keyboard and peering into a screen.

"What about the *Tourer*?" he asked. "Any word?"

"About sixty minutes out, Mr. Gaona. How about that coffee? Refill?"

He got it. She liked him. It often happened, though Marcel had no idea what the attraction was since he always found himself—in any mirror—quite plain-looking with a bullet-hole scar along his cheek. Maybe it was his warm personality, he thought with a laugh. Not.

"Yes, more coffee would be wonderful."

She came out from behind her desk. "By the way, while you were asleep the *Tourer* watch called in to report its scheduled maintenance. So I asked to speak with your Richard Dotty when I finished with the watch details. He came on the phone, and I told him about you with your news from his ex-wife in Miami. He didn't seem all that excited to know what it was about. In fact, he didn't say much at all. But he knows you're waiting. Do you take it black or were you going easy on me, Mr. Gaona?"

She said this last part as she was leaving the room. When she turned back around for his reply, there was no one there.

Emanuel Gaona, aka Marcel Rainford, was gone.

Chapter 33

MICHAEL

It was Marcel calling me. Mrs. Lingscheit knew to put him right through. I got up from my desk where I'd been interviewing a potential client and stepped down the hall into the library where I took Marcel's call.

"Marcel? This is Michael," I said.

"So effing close you wouldn't believe it, boss. He was on the next boat due into port; then a nosy Nellie ran him off for me. Son of a bitch, I was close."

"You sure it was him?"

"He's connected with heroin and doesn't have a ring finger. A mate told me all about him."

"What's his name?" I said.

"Richard Dotty is what he was going by," Marcel said. "'Course that's all changed by now. And I'm sure Dotty isn't his real name, either. Easy come, easy go."

"So what now?"

"I've been in touch with a friend at Interpol. She's going to look into it for me."

"She's an Interpol agent?"

"She is. An old friend."

I knew enough not to push it. Marcel had told me all he was going to say to me about her, but I was dying to know. Ex-girlfriend? Lover? Even a wife? I'd never find out. That much I was sure of.

"By the way, I learned something about you," I said conspiratorially.

Except he wasn't buying it. His tone told me we were not co-conspirators.

"Cough it up, Michael. What did you learn?"

"A certain Mrs. Lingscheit might have a crush on you."

"Our Mrs. Lingscheit? At our office?"

"Yes."

"Oh, for fuck's sake, Michael. I wouldn't touch a married woman with a ten-foot pole."

"It might not take all of that, Marce. She's quite smitten with you."

He abruptly shifted gears. "I'm probably headed to Europe or South America next. How's my funding for this caper?"

"Finding Nine Fingers? We're doing sixty over here. You'll have all the money you need."

"That old lady means a lot to you, eh?"

"Aunt Martha means everything to me, Marcel. She wouldn't complain about it if it weren't wearing terribly on her. She's much tougher than that. She survived a Japanese prison camp in the Philippines during World War Two. Some son of a bitch with a missing finger is nothing next to that. But for her, something is after her. She is horrified. She hasn't been able to sleep but an hour or two at a time ever since. I want this guy for her. Screw what it costs, Marcel. Bring him back to Chicago."

"You want him how?"

"How?"

"Dead or alive?"

"Alive. I want the bastard to suffer for what he did. Let him suffer by not knowing his execution date on death row. He deserves worse."

"I'm sure worse could be arranged. Just a few bucks needed, and I can put some pipe-carrying, ass-busting pain merchants on his white ass. You follow me?"

"Nothing would make me happier. Or Aunt Martha."

"I'll bring him back, Michael. And it's not going to take all that long, either. I promise."

"You're feeling that sure? Excellent, then. Do it."

"S'long, Michael. They're calling my flight."

"Where to?"

"Bogotá."

"Colombia? How do you know?"

"Just got a text. Paris number. One word, 'Bogotá.' She's given me my marching orders."

"Bye, Marcel."

The line was already dead.

Back to my office, I hurried.

Back to the real world of cops and robbers and courts.

While Marcel, somewhere in the air over Panama, chased Will-o'-the-Wisps all the way down to Bogotá.

* * *

Tocumen International (Panama City) to El Dorado International (Bogotá) flying time was precisely ninety minutes. Marcel sat in first class, a glass of wine balanced on his knee, slowly sipping, for the entire flight. The sun hadn't been up but a couple of hours and the morning air was smooth and colorful.

After landing at Bogotá, he made his way to the customs desk where he asked to speak to a supervisor.

His Interpol ID, which he hadn't turned in when leaving Interpol, was flashed in the supervisor's direction.

"I need to see all incoming manifests since four this morning, Mr. Ortega," Marcel explained.

"Certainly, Agent Gaona. Please have a seat in the outer office, and I'll have someone bring those out to you." Marcel's Interpol name was Gaona. Or was it Marcel? Sometimes it was a puzzle to remember all the old identities.

Marcel selected the closest seat to the door, put his back against the wall, and waited. What he was doing was a major crime in any country if he was caught flashing a void Interpol ID.

Estrella, his Interpol contact, had been spot on. Richard Dotty arrived two hours earlier from Panama City on Flight 1159. Marcel thanked the helpful people at Colombia Customs El Dorado and found his way outside the airport.

He'd been in Bogotá many times, most often during the heyday of the Colombia Cartel during the Escobar Eighties. Pablo Escobar, when Interpol had tracked him down, was bringing in $29 billion per year with his cocaine cartel. Marcel had been present the day he died, the day of the shootout in the streets of Bogotá just three weeks before Marcel was to return to Paris for Christmas. That was December 3, 1993. Marcel had refused the rotation back home; he was hot on the drug lord's trail and was set to bring him down personally. But Colombian joint forces, military, and Bogotá police, with assistance from Interpol and the DEA, got to him before Marcel made contact. When Marcel happened upon the scene of the Escobar assassination, he immediately turned and left for the airport. His female friend in Paris had a six-year-old son to whom Marcel had promised an electric train for Christmas. It had been time to make good on that promise, and so he did.

After landing in Bogotá, outside at the taxi stand, along the front of El Dorado International, Marcel began going taxi to taxi, carefully soliciting information about a gringo with a missing finger whom they might've taken away that morning. As each cab roared forward in line for the next fare, another would take its place at the end of the line, and Marcel would repeat his description and questions.

It was a long shot, but police work was often just that: long shots. He knew that, if he got lucky, he would quickly locate his quarry. When he did, and he was sure he would, who could say what might happen? Nine Fingers might make it back to Chicago, and then again, he might not. Marcel harbored no feelings about the man, but he also had only a very slight interest in prolonging the guy's life for a trial. That was my gambit, not Marcel's. Still, loyal as he was, he had promised to return the killer to the States, and for that reason alone, he would. It was called loyalty, and loyalty was at Marcel's center.

A full hour into his taxicab questions, Marcel met a Paki driver. Marcel asked him the three key questions:

1. Have you seen this guy? (Marcel would describe him)
2. Where did you take him?
3. What did he say to you?

The driver answered, "Yes, I saw him. I took him to Finca Del Sur. He didn't say a word."

"Where is Finca Del Sur?"

"Just off downtown."

"Let's go."

"Hop in, mister. There's a twenty-dollar gratuity for this service."

Marcel tossed a hundred-dollar bill over the seat. "Here's the fare and gratuity. Keep it all, but let's move it!"

They arrived ten minutes later at Avenida Boyacá and went south just beyond to Los Legatos lake. A quick left onto Calle 117, and shortly after came the intersection with Finca Del Sur. The driver pulled over just beyond a duplex made of stylized adobe, commercial grade stuff. He had purposely had the driver pull several units beyond the duplex where the driver said he'd left the fare that morning.

Marcel quickly climbed out and went around to the driver's open window. "Five-hundred

USD if you wait here and take my passenger and me back to the airport when I return here. Just ask no questions."

The Paki driver smiled a broad, toothy smile. "No questions. I'll be right here."

Marcel circled the duplex, into the backyard where a clutch of Rhode Island Red hens was pecking at freshly scattered seed on the ground. He stepped over the chicken wire and made his way to the back door. He waited there, listening. Then he crept around to the front door and quickly rang the bell before exploding into a dash for the back door.

Standing just beside the door, he made it with a second to spare. The door flew open, and a thin blond man came dashing outside. Marcel extended his leg, tripping the guy, then leaped on his prostrate body and rendered him unconscious with a carotid artery pressure point. Then he jerked the man's left arm out from under him and examined the left hand. Three fingers, one thumb. Missing ring finger.

Handcuffed to Marcel, the man in the backseat of the taxi slowly recovered consciousness. His first impulse was to break free and run, but Marcel slapped him across both knees with a lead sap before the commotion broke out. He groaned and fell forward, dangling there by the handcuff that linked him to Marcel.

Marcel nodded approvingly. "We're going to Chicago, Mr. Dotty. As you know, you're wanted there. If you're extra careful, special good, you might make it there alive. If you're not, why I'll crush your head in with my sap."

Marcel snapped the weapon again, this time catching the fugitive behind the head, just below the brain stem, knocking him unconscious yet again.

The ride to the airport was uneventful. Each time the man started to come around, Marcel snapped the lead sap across his head and sent him to la-la land again.

"Ouch!" said the driver into the mirror.

"Five-hundred USD, my friend. No questions, no comments, please."

From the entrance to the Bogotá airport all the way to O'Hare in Chicago, none of the authorities questioned Marcel and his prisoner once they were shown the Interpol ID. It was magic, opening doors and eliminating questions every mile of the way.

They landed in Chicago, after layovers one and two, almost twenty-four hours later. It had been a hellacious trip, but Marcel was up for anything. Even up to the point where he called me and asked where I wanted the prisoner delivered, Marcel was still considering eliminating the man. Marcel had little faith in the American Judicial System, and many times over the last twenty-four hours, he weighed the pros and cons of bypassing the trial and going straight to the sentence of death by aggravated assault and battery. But he didn't; he'd given me his word.

"Where do I take him, boss?"

"Will he talk?" I asked over the cell phone.

"Tell the truth. I don't know. But they'll always talk anyway, boss, if that's what you want."

"I want his recorded confession to the murders. If the police get the confession, a good defense lawyer might keep it from in front of the jury. But if a private citizen gets the confession, it's good as gold. There's no way to keep it out if it's given to me and you."

"So where do you want him?"

"Bring him to my condo."

"You sure, boss? This guy's a sicko. You sure you want him knowing where you live?"

"He could find that out anyway if he's set free, Marcel. You know how easy that is. No, bring him here. I'll be waiting."

"Roger that, boss. We'll be there in thirty minutes."

"The door's unlocked."

Chapter 34

MICHAEL

Marcel called me from O'Hare.

He had our man handcuffed and was bringing the killer to my condo. It was time to get the guy to confess to the murder of all those poor young nurses. I had been headed down to the office, but I turned around, went back inside, and changed into jeans and a T-shirt.

I grabbed rubber gloves from beneath the sink—for Marcel to wear, not me—just in case he needed them. Then I went into my hallway linen closet and selected a plain white king-size bedsheet. I spread the sheet in the center of the great room. Then I anchored it on all corners with a dining chair. The fifth dining chair was placed in the center of the bedsheet. I then covered it with the bottom sheet from the same set as the top sheet. I hadn't practiced law all those years and learned nothing about covering my tracks. I retrieved my Canon from the closet shelf in the master bedroom and mounted it on a tripod fifteen feet away from the centered chair. I switched it on and focused on the chair where Mr. Murder would be sitting while I filmed him.

I then removed two wall-hangings so they wouldn't show up in the background of the video. Using readily available enhancement techniques, any primary police crime lab in the country could draw into focus any purposely blurred backgrounds. But without the wall hangings, the criminologists could be looking at any of one-hundred-million great room walls in America. Track that down, friends.

Just as I finished making my preparations, the front door behind me swung open sharply. Here was Marcel, his copy of my condo's card key in hand, his left wrist manacled to his prisoner's right wrist. There was a size differential between the two men that should have made the smaller man, the killer, think twice about trying to overwhelm his captor.

"Let me see this guy," I said as soon as the door shut again. "I want to look a dead man right in the eye. Hey! Yes, you! I'm talking to you, asshole!"

The gray-haired guy just looked at me. Then he sneered at me.

"You're lucky I'm the nice guy here," I said to him just as I brought my fist up from my side and caught him on the side of the head. He crumpled to his knees. "As I said, pal, I'm Mr. Nice. Now, do you want to tell us your name?"

On his knees, yet, still swinging his head from side-to-side, he mumbled, "Go fuck yourself."

This time it was Marcel who pounced. He brought his lead sap down with brutal force against the guy's trapped right hand. I could hear the bones snapping from several feet away from where I was about to witness a down-home good time. At that point, I surprised myself. Call it bloodlust, call it revenge: I didn't give a rat's ass if this mass murderer died right there on my great room floor or a year from now in a gas chamber. I was out of patience.

Marcel jerked him to his feet and half-dragged him to the centered chair. Then he forced him into a sitting position before removing the handcuff from his own wrist. He dropped the man's cuffed arm down to his side and closed the open end of the cuffs around the bottom bracing of the chair. With great forethought, I could tell.

"Turn on your camera, Michael," Marcel whispered. "We'll edit out the vomit scenes."

"Vomit scenes?"

"The things I'm about to do to this asshole would make a jury vomit. Now, get me a steak knife."

I hurried in and returned with a steak knife, the kind with the serrated edge.

"Come over here, Michael. Unzip Mr. Happy's trousers."

"What?"

"Unzip his pants. I need access to his Johnson."

"His penis."

"Same difference, Michael."

"Hold it, Marcel. What're you going to do?"

"Circumcise our boy here. We'll see how he likes the blade in his flesh, just like he did to those poor girls."

"He cut their—their—"

"Their genitals. Didn't you read the police reports Aunt Martha gave us? I did. It seems like Mr. Happy mutilated every one of those young girls. Now it's his turn. Only he doesn't get to have his throat cut first."

"Marcel, come out here. We need to talk."

Into the hallway we stepped, closing the door behind us.

"Look," I said, "a confession obtained like this would never be allowed in court. There has to be some other way."

Marcel's eyes glared at me in the dim hallway light.

"You said you wanted a confession, boss. This guy won't even begin to confess unless I cut him. I've known too many just like him."

"How about you try everything else first and then we talk again before you cut him?"

"Hey, it's your circus. If you say."

"I say."

We went back inside and Marcel headed for his prisoner.

"What the hell?" said the blond man, speaking for the first time since being slammed down onto the chair by Marcel.

Marcel sapped the man on the side of the head. A smear of blood appeared from inside his ear.

"Whoops, popped an eardrum there? Sorry, pal!" Marcel shouted. "I say, old sport, can you hear me? Do you read lips?"

I realized just then that Marcel was training the man to believe that he meant nothing to Marcel, that Marcel could just as easily sap him or cut him as not. It worked, too. For the first time, Dotty's eyes flashed in fear. He was afraid of Marcel. Hell, by then, so was I.

He suddenly stepped forward and, inserting the knife with a quick twist, cut away the front of the man's Jockey shorts. Now his penis was fully exposed, flaccid and gray.

"Give me the gloves," Marcel demanded of me.

I couldn't hold back. "Didn't we just discuss this, Marcel?"

"Yes."

"You're going to actually cut the guy?"

"Yes," Marcel said with a wink only I could see. There it was: we were faking bloodwork. All right, then.

I handed the yellow gloves to him. I could feel an overwhelming fear grip me in the gut just then. I wanted to run; I wanted to hide. I realized how weak I was compared to this man I'd hired. Marcel took the yellow gloves, studied them, then pulled them on, snapping the wrists when he was satisfied.

"Now turn away," he said softly. "You won't want to see this."

* * *

Ten minutes later, Marcel came into my bedroom, asking me to leave my laptop and return to the great room with him. Which I did.

The first thing, the really obvious thing, was the large red half-moon bloodstain at the front of the prisoner's chair. I noticed his pants were zipped up again, but there was a new bloodstain spreading around the fly. I lifted my eyes to Dotty's face. No damage there. Evidently Marcel wanted him looking untouched in the video we were about to make.

"Our friend says he wants to confess," Marcel announced grandly. "I told him we could make that happen for him. Before he gets clipped again. Right now he's missing only half a load, thanks to my kindness. But he knows he could lose another half, and that would be it."

I didn't strictly understand the references but figured full comprehension wasn't critical to my role. The truth was, this was way beyond anything I'd bargained for. Or was it? Hadn't I all but promised Aunt Martha I'd kill the guy for her? So why the hesitation over Marcel's tune-up?

"Get behind your camera, Michael. Let's see what Mr. Murder has to say. Ready, Mr. Murder?"

"Uh-huh," the man grunted through bloodless, white lips.

"Okay, Michael, start filming…now!"

Then he pointed at Dotty, who began reading from a yellow legal pad."

"My name is Richard Sullivan Dotty. I am sixty-six years old. I don't have a regular address because I work at sea, and I'm always en route."

He looked up, making eye contact with Marcel. Marcel pointed at the yellow tablet.

"In 1966, I murdered a bunch of student nurses in Chicago. They were all Filipino. I cut their throats and watched them die. I planned their murders. I knew that night after I left the tavern that I was angry and wanted to kill someone. Anyone would do. When I climbed the fire escape and looked inside the building, I knew I wanted to kill the people I saw, and so I did."

He then held up his free hand, his left hand, to the camera.

"One survivor has identified the killer as a man missing the ring finger on his left hand. Look at this. See that? No ring finger. I lost it to a barge bowline when I was eighteen-years-old. Traumatic amputation. The court refused to award me any money for my finger. I've been crazy angry ever since."

He stopped and looked at Marcel, who made a wind-it-up motion with his hand. The captive then dropped his eyes back to the legal pad and read, "I have given this statement today voluntarily and of my own volition. Nobody has coerced me. Nobody has threatened me with physical harm. Nobody has caused me physical harm or injury. I am not under any form of coercion. That is all I have to say. Thank you."

I switched off the camera.

"Brilliant!" Marcel exclaimed to the man who'd just starred in his own death warrant. "Nicely done, Mr. Dotty. Oh, nicely done!"

"I need water."

"Oh, no, lad, no water for you. Not for twenty-four hours. If you have water tonight and have to urinate, you'll only start bleeding again. We can't have that, now, can we." It was rhetorical, not a question.

Dotty looked down at his crotch. He buried his chin in his chest and shut his eyes.

"What now, Marcel?" I asked.

"I'll drive him to jail. He'll be booked. He'll never see the light of day again."

"Can you promise that to you-know-who?"

"Your aunt? I can, indeed."

"Then please take him and go. I have cleaning up to do."

"It all gets burned, Michael."

"I know."

"Does your building have a furnace room?"

It was an old building. "It does."

"Use that. Dump Mr. Happy's things in the furnace room and stoke it up."

"How do you avoid being arrested for hurting him, Marcel?"

"Don't worry about that. No one will ever know."

"He knows."

"Oh, but he's promised he won't talk. I've let him keep one-half of his package for his silence. He knows I can reach inside any prison any time I want and harvest the other half. He won't talk. Right, Mr. Happy?"

"Right."

"Smile when you say that."

"Right."

Smiling.

Smiling through the pain.

Chapter 35

MICHAEL

The Monday after Thanksgiving, in 2012, the trial of Richard Dotty began.

I addressed the jury first after they had been selected, sworn, and seated in the box.

"Ladies and gentlemen, my name is Michael Gresham, and I represent the people of the State of Illinois in this prosecution of Richard Dotty."

How did I happen to be prosecuting Dotty? My father was a prosecutor the night the murders occurred. He was called out to the crime scene shortly after the police arrived. He spoke to witnesses that night and even filed his own report. So, the State's Attorney's office was conflicted out because one of its own—albeit an ex-employee—cannot be a witness and the SA's office prosecute the same case. That being the case, a rationale existed for me to walk in and take over the prosecution—on my father's recommendation and request to his bosses. They agreed, based on my reputation, which was quite convincing by then. Not to mention that I had prosecuted for years in the Army, so the State's Attorney knew he wasn't getting a virgin.

It was just that simple. So, there I was, about to make my opening statement to the jury.

First off, I slowly and reverently read the names of each student nurse murdered that Thanksgiving night in 1966. Then I started in. "None of the victims knew Richard Dotty. None of his victims had done anything to Dotty or anyone else that would bring down this wrath on them.

"But this is my chance to tell you what the evidence, in this case, will show. First, that the victims were innocent. Second, that Richard Dotty killed them just to watch them die. Third, that Richard Dotty showed no remorse. And fourth, that Richard Dotty planned this crime ahead of time and he broke into that dorm with the intention of committing murder. All of which will prove that Richard Dotty should be convicted of premeditated murder.

"The State's first witness will be Cleveland Gresham, who is my father. Why is he a witness in my case? Because on Thanksgiving Day in 1966, he was a prosecutor at the Cook County State's Attorney's Office and because of that, he was called to the crime scene the night it happened. The evidence will show that he spoke to one witness, in particular, the only living person who remained after the killings occurred. She told Cleveland Gresham that night what she observed about the killer. She will tell you those same exact data points when she testifies here as the State's second witness.

"Our second witness will be a woman named Martha Bautista. She is a nurse who was there the night of the slayings. She will tell you what she saw and heard. She will testify about the killer's missing ring finger. She will tell you about setting off the alarms that summoned the police and EMTs."

I didn't bother to reveal that I was "related" to Aunt Martha. What they didn't know wouldn't hurt them. Martha, likewise, had been coached not to muddy the waters with that information. It wasn't crucial to the case, and I didn't want to be accused later of calling my relatives as witnesses. That would never do. So I left it at my father, and that was that. No nepotism involved.

"The State will then call a series of police officers and detectives. They will tell you the who, what, where, why, and when of the case. They will talk about what each of them did at the scene and who they spoke with and what they observed. Finally, the detectives will testify about Richard Dotty's video of him confessing. Dotty himself will tell you he was confessing voluntarily without threat, without injury or pain, and without coercion. Very compelling, let me say.

"The State will then call a series of crime scene investigators. They will talk about footprints, fingerprints, and all the other evidence they collected from the scene. The photographer and videographer will testify and show you still photographs of the scene and the victims as they were found that night by the officers answering the alarm. The videographer will also walk you through the crime scene room-by-room and show you the bodies of each victim and the wounds indicating how they were killed.

"The State will then call the medical examiner, and she will testify about wounds, what the wounds indicate, and causes of death, as well as autopsy reports on each body. Why do we need to review the autopsies with you, a particularly gruesome commentary? Because, for one, we need to know how and why each nurse died. Equally important, we must prove to you that the victims died, not from natural causes or disease processes, but because of the wounds inflicted by Richard Dotty.

"We will then call family members and friends who will tell you about each of the victims.

"After our case is complete, I expect the defendant, Richard Dotty, not to testify. He has nothing to say—absolutely nothing—that will aid his attorneys in defense of his case. Instead, his testimony would only serve to make his role in the murders that much more obvious. I also have his written confession to the crimes, as mentioned previously, and I'll ask him about that, should he choose to testify."

Then I wrapped up with the usual admonitions and request for guilty verdicts and took my seat.

It was time for the defense to present its opening statement.

It was time for the defense to explain why Richard Dotty shouldn't be found guilty of multiple counts of First Degree Murder.

Now, I never liked to predict the outcome of my trials. I'd learned that once you go before a jury, anything could happen. That was true because when you went before a jury, the case slipped from your fingers, out of your control. So the fact that I had Dotty's video confession in my file as I stood at the lectern that first morning did very little to assuage my nervous anticipation. As I said, anything could happen, and I damn well knew it.

Plus, there was the matter of how the confession was obtained. If the jury believed the confession, a guilty verdict was all but automatic. But if they didn't believe it...I'd seen cases where the jury got angry about how the confession was coerced and ignored the rest of the evidence, turning the defendant loose.

Which brings me to the matter of the bloodstains on the confession. They were unexplainable. So I decided to use my prosecutorial discretion and shitcan the written confession. I would rely on the video only.

* * *

I opened the State's case by calling, as my first witness, my father, Cleveland Gresham.

"State your name."

"Cleveland Gresham."

"Mr. Gresham, what is your occupation?"

"I'm a lawyer. I have my law practice."

"Did you at one-time work for the Cook County State's Attorney's Office?"

"I did. I was an Assistant State's Attorney there."

"Were you employed there during the murders of the student nurses?"

"I was."

"Directing your attention to November 24, 1966, what, if anything, occurred that night?"

"A mass murder. That's what happened."

"Tell us your role in the investigation of that case, please."

"I was the State's Attorney on-call for major crimes that night. When the phone rang, I answered. I was needed at the crime scene, so I hurried right over."

"Tell us what you saw when you arrived there."

"Tell you who I saw?"

"General impressions first, please."

"There were marked and unmarked CPD police cars everywhere. The dormitory is across the street from Roosevelt Hospital."

"That would be on Greenleaf Road?"

"Yes."

"That would be in Cook County, Illinois?"

"Yes."

"Please proceed with what you saw."

"As I said, vehicles everywhere. I parked almost all the way at the end of the block and started walking. It was starting to snow, so I was wearing my parka with my hood up and lined gloves on my hands. The sky was overcast, of course, and there was no moonlight. As I walked along, I didn't pass any other person. At the entrance, I showed my ID."

"Your State's Attorney ID?"

"Yes. They let me through without a question. I then proceeded upstairs."

"How did you get upstairs?"

"Stairway. The elevator was shut down. They told me later the crime scene guys were in the elevator running their vacuums. They were looking for hair and fiber. The trace and transfer people were in there, too, dusting for prints."

"All right, we'll come back to those findings later. What floor did you climb to?"

"Second floor. When I got there, the door was taped off with yellow crime scene tape. I badged the uniform at the door, and he let me through."

"He took down the tape from the doorway?"

"Yes, just long enough to let me pass through."

"What did you see there?"

"The hallway was cordoned off right down the center. You could only pass through on the inside wall side of the tape. When I got closer, I could see why."

"Why was it cordoned off?"

"Because there were bloody footprints everywhere."

"Did you learn whose footprints they were?"

"I learned that the killer left some, but most of them were first responders. There were also footprints left by the sole survivor. I believe they told me she ran from room to room after the killer was gone, checking if anyone was alive."

"Did you know any of the people in the hallway?"

"I did. I knew Detective Frank McMillan. He was directing traffic in the hallway, preserving the scene until the CSI finished with the elevators. He was also talking to other students from downstairs who had come upstairs to see what was going on before the police arrived."

"Did you speak with any of the civilians?"

"I did. I asked several of them if they'd seen or heard anything."

"What did they tell you?"

"Objection! Hearsay."

The objection had been made by Dotty's defense attorney, a particularly shrewd attorney from LaSalle Street named Rusk Levin. Mr. Levin was well-known in criminal law circles of Chicago. He was older, maybe even in his seventies, and he'd tried hundreds of jury trials. His Yellowpage ad claimed he was an expert in criminal law and that he was certified in criminal law by the NBLSC. Over the past several months, as we worked up the case and defended against his dozens of pre-trial motions, I had come to know Mr. Levin as a brilliant combatant who had no fear of any judge or lawyer. He didn't hesitate to raise hell when he thought Dotty was being taken advantage of by the system or the prosecution. He even threatened several times to turn me into the Bar Association for imaginary wrongs. I told him to go right ahead. I also told him to screw himself, but my language wasn't that polite.

When Levin objected to the hearsay I was soliciting from the witness, the judge peered down at me. "Counsel?" she asked.

"I'll withdraw the question, Your Honor."

"Very well."

"Mr. Gresham, did you ever come across any eyewitness?"

"Only one."

"What was that person's name."

"Martha Bautista."

"Did you talk to Martha Bautista that night?"

"I did."

"Without telling us what she said, can you tell us what you learned during that talk?"

"She didn't see the killer's face. But she saw his left hand. She saw he was missing his ring finger on that hand."

"If you know, what did Martha Bautista see that night?"

"Objection! Foundation."

"He's right, counsel," said the judge. "For you to prove what she saw, you're going to need to demonstrate her ability to see and perceive accurately, as well as her opportunity to see and hear. In other words, what was her vantage point? Was there adequate light to see by? Was her vision good? You know what I need to hear, Mr. Gresham. Objection sustained."

I was going to need to call Aunt Martha as a witness and get her story. How was that going to work, me being related to two of the witnesses in the case? Technically, I wasn't actually related to Martha, so there was that. But Rusk Levin was going to hammer the hell out of the fact we were longtime acquaintances and friends. That was a problem for another day.

So I circled back around to the witness, who wasn't going to be able to tell the jury anything about Martha Bautista.

"Did you observe the victims that night?"

"I did. All of them."

"Tell us what you remember about that."

"It's been a long time. I'll do my best."

"Please do."

"I went inside two rooms. In the first one, there were four beds composed of two sets of bunk beds. Detective Elias Ellingson took me to view each bed and its occupant. First, they were all female. Second, they all had the same type of wound."

"What wounds did they have?"

"Their throats had been slit from ear to ear."

I paused and pretended to be shuffling through my notes at that point. I was letting that "throats slit ear to ear" soak in with the jury. It was a nice mental graphic. "Mr. Gresham, I'm going to show you a set of photographs to review. When you have gone through them all, I'm going to ask whether the photos are true and accurate portrayals of what you saw that night. Can you remember enough to confirm the photos for us?"

"I think so. I won't know for sure until I see them."

"Well, did anyone show you any photos before your testimony here today?"

"No. I haven't seen any crime scene photos since 1966."

"Very well."

I then obtained the court's permission to present a handful of photographs to the witness for review. The court called a stretch break so everyone could run pee while my witness reviewed the photographs. Standard operating procedure, so far. Which was what I wanted. I had no desire at all to have unique matters come up in the trial, matters that could create grounds for the witness to appeal. Rusk Levin, of course, would be doing everything he could to create unique moments for appeal. That's what defense lawyers are supposed to do.

We resumed about ten minutes later. The court allowed me to pass the photographs to the jury. There were cries of "Oh, no!" from many jurors, and one woman suddenly stood and ran for the restrooms. Another break in the evidence while she threw-up her breakfast. Then we resumed again.

Shortly after a line of fairly innocuous questions by me, Rusk Levin then took Cleveland through a not-so-bad cross-examination. There wasn't much he could ask an after-event witness. In fact, the more he went after Cleveland, the more precise the death scene became in everyone's minds, as well as the fatal wounds and the like. Levin eventually backed off after he'd done more damage to his client than to the State.

We took our afternoon break.

Chapter 36

MICHAEL

My mother, Wendy Gresham, was an honest woman. She instilled that same honesty in Arnie and me. She worked hard, too, at that sometimes impossible task as Arnie and I were growing up and running the scams on our parents that most boys try out at one time or other. My father, Cleveland, was an honest man, but his emphasis was on logic and reason when dealing with Arnie and me. He was the abstract thinker, the philosopher; our mother was the hands-on mechanic in charge of our souls. Honesty and logic—those were the keys to thriving in our family.

When I was very young, I accompanied my mother to Sprouse-Reitz, a store known as the "dime store." She was there to purchase a bobbin for her Singer sewing machine; I was there to obtain a box of caps for my cap gun. Like I said, I was very young—cap gun age.

When it was time to go through checkout, my mother steered me to the front of the store. Now, she had already told me we weren't there to buy toys for me. She had already told me I wasn't along for acquisitions. I was along because I was too young to leave at home. It was a school day, and I'd complained of a stomach ache that morning to buy myself a day off from school. In thinking about it, it was probably my rapid recovery from my sore throat that had doomed me to no toys at the dime store. Not even a box of caps. So, when we met together at the checkout line, the box of caps that I coveted, and needed very desperately, was tucked away in the right front pocket of my Levi's. Standing there in line, no taller than my mother's elbow, I suddenly realized the caps were burning a hole in my jeans. Not literally, but my sense of right and wrong—thanks to my mother—convicted me on the spot of the terrible crime I was about to commit of shoplifting the caps. I even touched the outside of my pants covering the caps to make sure there wasn't any real fire happening down there. As we went through the checkout line and exited at the end of the counter, I was all but gasping for air in my hyperventilated state.

"What's wrong with you?" my mother asked when we made it outside.

"I'm hot. Maybe I have a fever."

She laid the back of her hand on my forehead. "No, you're not hot. What else do you think it might be?"

"I don't know."

"Are you sure you don't know?"

"No, I don't know."

"Well let me ask you this. What is it you have in your pocket that's making it bulge out?"

"It is? I don't know."

"Well, let's look. Turn your pocket inside-out, Michael. Maybe we'll both learn something."

That moment, the feeling that swarmed over me like madness was the same feeling I had the first morning of the Dotty trial when I was explaining to the jury that I had, in my file, the video confession of Richard Dotty himself. Feelings don't change, only circumstances do.

Describing the confession to the jury, I could feel my mother's eyes on me.

When I finished my opening statement to the jury that first morning of trial, a moment of hyperventilation almost knocked me off my feet as I walked back to my table.

The confession was going to be a problem. How it had been obtained might even be enough to set a mass murderer free once the jury found out.

My pockets were about to turn inside-out.

* * *

My first police witness was Detective Frank Gillman, a hale and hearty fifty-something on the verge of retirement or heart attack from obesity, whichever came first. He was a good guy, but he was totally out-of-shape and breathing heavily when he took the witness stand and raised his right hand. Yes, he said, he swore to tell the truth.

The first day had ended when Levin finished up his cross-examination of Cleveland, and then I poked around with re-direct for a half-hour or so. I wish I could say I managed to squeeze more facts out of my father, the witness, but it wouldn't be true. We mainly just rehashed his direct examination, and then the judge recessed us for the day.

Detective Gillman waited calmly while I gathered up my papers and headed for the lectern to begin my direct examination of him.

"State your name."

"Francis S. Gillman. I go by 'Frank.' Or 'detective.'"

"Detective Gillman, you work for the Chicago PD, correct?"

"Yessir. I've just about got my twenty."

"Twenty years?"

"Yessir. I'm retiring in six months."

"Really? Then what?"

"Largemouth bass, Blue Gill, Lake Michigan—who knows what else?"

"Good luck with all of that. Now, directing your attention to this case involving the murder of the seven student nurses. Did you happen to be on the scene of the murder at any time, including the night of the event itself?"

"No, sir. I picked the case up after it went cold for many years."

"How did that come about that you picked it up, as you put it?"

"My lieutenant makes my case assignments. He sent me a memo."

"But what prompted him to do that?"

"Our office received a confession in the email."

"How did that happen?"

The detective shrugged. "Dunno. It just showed up in the CPD general email. Someone spotted it and sent it to Lieutenant Eivers."

"And he sent the case—and the confession—to you?"

"That's correct."

"What about the confession, is it video, written, what?"

"It's a video."

"Did it come with the name of the person who sent it?"

"No, it was sent from the city library's computer bank. Someone went to the library and sent it by email so it couldn't be traced."

"Did you try to trace it?"

"I did."

"What did you find out?"

"I found out the library doesn't keep a log of who uses its computers. They're open to the public on a first-come basis. No records are kept, and the Wi-Fi is a public one, no need to log in."

"Did you take any other steps in trying to locate who sent the video confession?"

"I did. I had the FBI crime lab review the tape. They said—"

"Objection! Hearsay."

I responded to Levin's objection. "Not hearsay, Your Honor. It's being offered only to prove what was said, not the truth of what was said."

"Overruled. You may continue."

"What were you told by the FBI, Detective?" I asked again.

"They said there were no identifying characteristics. It contained nothing that would direct them to any videographer. They even enhanced the background of the video so they could see the wall behind Dotty when he was confessing. But the wall didn't show anything."

"All right. Now, I'm going to ask that you play the video for the jury. Counsel and I have already discussed the video with the court, and it's been ruled that you may show it now."

"Yes, sir. All I have to do is click this control, and the video will play over the court's CCTV."

"Please click."

"Done."

The four courtroom flat screens jumped to life, beginning with a middle-distance view of Richard Dotty in my condo—of course, no one would ever know that location. A voice off-screen, modified by a simple voice-disguise app, began by asking Dotty to tell his name. Which he did. Then he was asked whether anyone was forcing him to confess. He gave a long, pained look at the camera, but ultimately shook his head and said, "No, he hadn't been forced, he hadn't been coerced, no one had beaten or injured him in any way."

The jury was taking down what was being said. When Dotty said the statement was freely given, many of the jurors relaxed a bit, even sat back in their chairs as the worry for what might be coming evaporated.

Ten minutes later, the screen went blank as Dotty again said he knew he was being videoed and it was all right, he hadn't been forced. In between, he had taken the jury on the full ride. They'd learned where he was the night of the murders, that he'd been drinking to intoxication, that he'd entered the dormitory with the intention of hurting someone—killing someone, even. He described killing the first roomful of sleeping nurses, then slipping down the hallway and killing again and again. He would've killed more, too, he allowed, if one nurse hadn't disappeared and was maybe off getting help. The video had ended, and the jury looked up at the judge when the lights came back up.

"Ladies and gentlemen," the judge said, "we'll take our morning break right here, and then Mr. Levin can begin his cross-examination of the witness."

It was 10:30 a.m. when we broke. Detective Gillman came straight over to my table after the jury was removed from the room. He wanted to know if he'd done okay, and I told him he'd done perfectly. He then went on out to use the bathroom.

Marcel, sitting beside me as a member of my trial team, caught my eye. He gave an almost imperceptible nod. I nodded back, and we went out into the hallway and put our heads together at the far end, where nobody from the court was anywhere near.

"He's going to call me as a witness. I can feel it," he said.

"If he does, he does. There's not much we can do about that, Marcel."

"But what if he asks about my role in the video. What do I say?"

"Tell the truth. Say you videoed the confession."

"But that's not the truth. You videoed it. I just asked the questions."

Just then, the bailiff stuck his head out the door and called to me. The judge wanted a word with counsel. I patted Marcel's shoulder and left for chambers.

"Counsel," Judge Mendoza said, "Attorney Levin has indicated to the court he plans to call your investigator to the stand to testify. For the record, please give us your position on that."

I thought about it for a moment, then, "I'd object, Judge, except I don't know what my grounds would be. I suppose he's entitled to examine the chief investigator."

"But isn't Mr. Rainford a private citizen?" said the Judge. "How could he be a police investigator?"

"He never served as a police investigator, Your Honor. He served as my private investigator. I paid him myself."

"Why would you do that?"

"Because my Aunt Martha asked me to find the killer. She was in one of the rooms the night of the murders. She hasn't slept since that night. She has PTSD. She wanted him arrested. So I paid my firm's private investigator since the CPD had closed the books on the investigation."

It was reasonable enough. The court and counsel already knew all about Martha Bautista. In fact, I had her listed as my next witness to be called. So her role was no surprise to anyone.

"I see," said Judge Mendoza. "Very well, I'll allow the defense to call your investigator once you've rested your case, counsel."

Levin and I nodded. It hadn't been a hot issue after all.

The court then called us back in session, and we were off and running again. It was then that I had the bright idea of calling Marcel as my witness first to take the wind out of Levin's sails and to avoid looking like I had something to hide.

Levin cross-examined Detective Gillman without much effect. The man hadn't been on the scene, and he'd mostly just reviewed the video like everyone else. Not much to be mined there at all.

Which was when I called Marcel Rainford as the State's next witness.

Marcel and I hadn't finished our conversation outside in the hallway. We hadn't covered and prepared for what Levin might ask. But there was no time at that point, so I launched into my direct examination of Marcel. After getting out his name, job, history as a cop and Interpol agent, we launched into his role on the Dotty case.

"Where did you first see Richard Dotty?"

"Bogotá, Colombia."

"What was his reason for being there?"

"He was a seaman on a steamer."

"On a ship?"

"That's right."

"How did you locate him?"

"By tracking down the name of his ship and then tracking it down. I waited for him to come ashore."

"What happened when he came ashore?"

"He tried to lose me. But I was able to follow. I then got him to come outside of the house where he'd gone. He came out, and we talked it over. Then he came back to Chicago with me."

"You flew with him back to Chicago?"

"Yes. He said he wanted to come straighten it all out."

"Did he resist coming to Chicago with you?"

"Not really. I mean, it wasn't on the top of his list of things to do, but he came anyway."

"Did you force him to come to Chicago?"

"Not really."

"What happened when you got to Chicago?"

"I set up a video session and recorded his confession."

"Is that your voice on the confession?'

"Yes, sir."

"Who all was there at the confession?"

"Just me, Dotty, and the guy running the video camera."

"Did Mr. Dotty speak freely into the camera and without coercion?"

"Well, yes and no."

"What does that mean?"

"He'd been injured previously and needed medical care. It wasn't an emergency, so I told him we'd go for medical care as soon as I had his confession."

"Did he get medical care that night?"

"Well, after he confessed I took him to the police."

"What happened there?"

"They said they didn't have any wants or warrants, so they turned him loose."

"Were you there when this happened, when they turned him loose?"

"I sure was."

"What happened next?"

"He needed a place to crash, so I took him back to my place."

"He stayed with you?"

"Yes."

"How long did he stay with you?"

"About a week."

"Then what happened?"

"I called the police station and said I had him. I spoke to someone, and they said yes, they had a new arrest warrant for Richard Dotty. So I took him to the police station. This time, they locked him up. I didn't see him again until this trial began."

"The Richard Dotty in this courtroom—is he the same man you located in Colombia?"

"Yes. The same man who accompanied me back to Chicago."

"The same man who confessed?"

"Yes."

Suddenly Rush Levin stood up and asked the court if counsel could approach. The court said we could, so Levin and I huddled with Judge Mendoza and kept our voices down.

"Your Honor," Levin whispered, "the witness is lying. My client is waiting to testify how this witness half-castrated him to make him talk."

"Come again?" said the judge.

"That's right. This witness cut off Mr. Dotty's right testicle with a steak knife."

Judge Mendoza looked over our heads, out at the jury, making sure they didn't hear any of this.

"Counsel, why is this the first time I'm hearing this?"

"Because I didn't hear about it myself until ten minutes ago when he whispered to me at counsel table. I just about fell out of my chair. So the defendant moves to suppress the video and moves for a mistrial. That video confession was coerced by physical injury and threats of another injury."

"Which was?"

"Marcel Rainford said he would take my client's other testicle if he didn't confess."

"Did he do that to your client?"

"No, he confessed instead."

"This needs to be reported to the police," Judge Mendoza said. "I'm going to halt the trial and take your client's testimony in my chambers, Mr. Levin. I assume he'll be willing to testify on the issue of coercion?'

"He will, Your Honor. It's the right thing to do."

By now, my heart was racing. My name hadn't come up yet, but I was sure that was only minutes away. I'd soon be under police investigation along with Marcel. I could already hear the two of us denying everything Dotty was about to tell the judge. We would be committing perjury. All of this insanity for Aunt Martha. I was kicking myself, asking over and over how I'd let this happen in my condo. What the hell had I been thinking?

* * *

Fifteen minutes later, we were all set up in the judge's office, complete with court reporter and clerk of the court. Levin was sitting directly in front of the judge, Dotty sat to his left, and I was on his right. The jury had been returned to the jury room.

"Please present your witness for examination," the judge told Levin.

Levin asked the clerk to swear him in, and then Levin began with his direct exam. "Mr. Dotty, did you hear Marcel Rainford just a half hour ago telling the jury about your confession?"

"I sure did."

"Did you hear him tell the jury that your confession was freely and voluntarily given?"

"Yes, I did."

"Was that the truth?"

"No, it was not."

"Tell us why you say that?"

"Because he clipped my nut to make me talk. Snip-snip!"

The men in the judge's chambers, including the judge and the bailiff, all winced and involuntarily pulled away from an imaginary knife headed for our crotches.

"Did he snip both your testicles?"

"No, just Little Boy."

"And who is Little Boy?"

I could tell Levin had never heard of Little Boy before. He was flying blind at this point just like the rest of us.

"Little Boy's the little nut. You know, the one on the right. He's the one got clipped."

"Were any steps taken to keep you from bleeding to death that night?"

"Oh, he just slit the sack and clipped me with a fingernail clipper. It didn't bleed all that much."

"Was it painful?"

"Well, shit, man, what do you think?"

"I don't want to think about it," Levin volunteered. "It's too painful to think about. But, moving ahead. You're telling the judge you agreed to confess to the murder of those student nurses in return for no more physical attack on your testicles?"

"That's right."

"For the record, Mr. Dotty, did you murder those student nurses?"

"Hell, no. What would I go and do something like that for? That's sick, sick, sick."

"One last request, please," Levin said, and I thought, oh, brother here it comes. It turns out I was right.

"Please stand and drop your drawers to show the judge the missing testicle."

"What the hell?" said Dotty. "How can I show him the missing testicle if it's gone? That don't compute."

"Please," the judge interjected. "Please allow the court to review your gonad sac."

"Suit yourself," Dotty said, and seconds later he was fully exposed in the genital area. I was watching the court reporter for some obtuse reason. Yes, she craned her head to have a look, too. I guess she needed to see it to put it on the record. As for me, a quick glance, then I looked away.

"Counsel," said Judge Mendoza to me, "do you have any questions?"

"I do," I said. "Mr. Dotty, that wound doesn't look recent to me. How do we know someone else didn't do this to you long before your confession and you're just using it now?"

"C'mon, Mr. Gresham. You were there when it happened. I saw you look."

"Hold it!" Judge Mendoza snarled. "Hold it right there. Mr. Gresham, were you, in fact, present when Mr. Dotty was assaulted and disfigured?"

My pockets had just been turned inside-out. I could hear my mother's voice outside the dime store. I've heard it many times since. The truth and I have become old friends. So I let go of the death hold I had on my case.

"I was. Not by choice, though. I didn't know it was coming until it was all over."

"Why were you even in the room at all?" the judge asked me.

"It was—it was my house. My condo. Marcel brought Mr. Dotty to my house after landing with him at O'Hare. He wanted to take a statement, and I supplied the camera."

"Were you the camera operator during the period of the confession?"

"I was."

"Did you do anything to prevent the castration of Mr. Dotty?"

"No."

"And knowing this had happened, and knowing his confession was coerced, you still decided to use the confession at this trial in my courtroom?"

'Yes."

I wanted the earth to open up and swallow me whole. I wanted to nail this murderous bastard so much because I had allowed it to progress to this point. Now I'd been found out. Now I was in deep, deep trouble.

"Counsel, Mr. Dotty's taped confession was testimonial. You knew it was perjury. You suborned perjury in my courtroom. That, sir, is a felony in this state. I'm going to recommend to the State's Attorney that both you and Marcel Rainford be prosecuted for your crimes in this matter. A mistrial is granted. Defendant shall be released on his own recognizance pending retrial. The defendant is confined to his home up to and including during retrial. Have I left anything out?"

"I get to go home?" Dotty stage-whispered to his lawyer.

Levin nodded. "No, Your Honor, nothing further."

The judge didn't wait for my response. He didn't give a damn about my response.

And I didn't blame him.

Part VI

Chapter 37

Knowles Gresham—Michael's grandfather—died in 1989 at the age of 90. But before he died, one giant lie was weighing heavily on his heart. It was the last wrong that he knew he was going to have to make right before he left the world. All of their lives, Roland and Cincy Knowles had lived with the belief that Natalia Gresham was their birth mother, which was a lie, a lie Natalia never told them. Only Knowles had ever lied to them. Now he knew, in his final days, slipping away in his bed at home where he was being cared for by a hospice team, he knew he had to make it right.

But how to make it right? What did that even mean?

Knowles called for Father Tom, his parish priest. He told the padre he wanted to make his confession before he died. The priest had visited in the Gresham household many times. He knew everyone there very well, including Martha Bautista. He didn't hesitate in answering Knowles's call to come for confession.

On that cold Christmas Eve day, Father Tom arrived on the elder Gresham's front porch. He was immersed in yards and yards of woolens, his defense against the cold that, in his words, "Surpasses all understanding." Father Tom was a Jesuit, educated at St. Louis University, with a good sense of irony that, when all else seemed to be going to hell, kept him in secret good spirits.

Knowles's housekeeper answered the door. She greeted Father Tom and led him straight upstairs to Knowles's bedside. He found the elder Gresham immobilized by his recent stroke, unable to speak except with great difficulty. The limbs on his right side were virtually useless, but he was able to lift a water glass with his left arm, though with considerable effort.

"Father," Knowles forced the word from his mouth, "thank you."

"You knew I'd come on a moment's notice, I hope. Last confessions are the second most important time in a person's life."

Knowles didn't care about all that; he wanted only to unburden himself. "Here's…the…thing."

"Yes. Go on."

"I have fathered three children."

"Yes, Roland and Cincy and Cleveland. I know them."

"The two older ones, Roland and Cincy. I've always told them their mother was Natalia."

"Of course, God rest her soul."

"Yes. Well, that's not the truth. The truth is Roland and Cincy were born to Martha Bautista. You know her; she was Natalia's nurse all those years in the iron lung."

"That must have caused Natalia untold pain."

"No…father. It was Natalia's…own idea."

"Well."

"But Natalia and I lied to the kids. We told them Natalia was their mother."

"But they must've been suspicious otherwise. They resemble Martha in her Filipino looks much more than they ever resembled Natalia. Don't you think they already know, now that they're grown?"

"Then that troubles me even more because that would mean…they know I was lying to them all their lives. They would know I still am. I can't die with that, father. I've got to be true to my children."

"And to yourself, I'd think. So…how can I help?"

"Forgive my sin, father, for I am a sinner."

"Do you repent?"

"I do."

"Then tell your children the truth and apologize to them. Your sins will be forgiven in this manner."

"I was afraid you'd say that."

"No, Knowles, you knew I'd say that. You were asking my blessing, not my permission."

"You know me well, Father Tom."

"I should. We've been priest and penitent many years now, Knowles. That's why I'm here before Mass tonight."

"How should I go about this, father?"

"Call them to your bedside. Tell them you've lied to them. Then tell them the truth. And whatever you do, don't try to excuse your sin, or justify it by all those reasons you found it necessary in the first place. They don't care about way back when. They only care about now."

"And what of Martha? Do I owe her an apology?"

"I think you do. Martha nearly gave up the chance to mother her children to protect your career, Knowles. She probably deserves your confession and apology more than anyone."

"I was afraid you might say that."

"No, I guess that deep down you're relieved to hear me say that, Knowles, because deep down you're a fine man."

"Thank you…father."

* * *

Martha dropped by that Christmas Eve to check up on Knowles. Christmas Eve was never complete without the visit from Martha. He expected and hoped for it every year.

That Christmas Eve, she sat beside his bed, staring at her immobile lover.

"Fine mess you've got yourself into, Knowles," she said with a lilt in her voice. Ever the nurse, Martha knew she wasn't going to see Knowles again. This would be their last time together. "So how does this go?" she asked. "What do we need to say?"

"I need to tell you I'm sorry, Martha. It should have been you."

"I won't argue. But it wasn't. You had made your choice while you thought the Japanese murdered me. But there's more to the story. I was raped by the Japanese rather than them killing me. I was their toy. In 1944, I gave birth at the prison camp. At first, the Japanese soldiers threatened to kill her. But they liked me and loved my body, which they used right up until she was born. So they relented and allowed me to keep her. She stayed alive on my milk until the Americans came. It was all I had to give her."

Knowles looked at her with his large gray eyes. She remembered when sometimes his eyes were blue. Most often after they had made love and the afternoon light was coming in through the window in his bedroom. Yes, then they were blue.

He swallowed hard, but a sliver of drool still ran out the side of his mouth onto his pillow. Martha took the corner of his sheet and wiped it away. Then he spoke. "Why didn't I ever get to meet your baby?"

She resolutely shook her head. "Don't you remember America after the war? Don't you remember the violent hatred of the Japanese? My daughter was more Japanese than Filipino. I couldn't bring her with me to America when I came back to find you. Instead, I left her with Ami. Ami became that child's mother and raised her from then on."

"Oh, my God. That means you lost all of your children to someone else."

Martha sat without moving. Her eyes filled with tears. She choked down a sob; it wouldn't be good for him to see how utterly destroyed she was by all that had happened. She wanted her final moments with Knowles to be happy ones and would do nothing to upset that. "Oh," she said matter-of-factly, "it wasn't all that. It was just life."

"But it was your life, my dear Martha."

She stood then and leaned across him. She placed the side of her face against his chest and shut her eyes. Just for those moments—those few seconds—he belonged to her again. And that's the way she wanted it remembered.

She lifted her head, then, and kissed him squarely on the mouth.

With a squeeze of his hand, Martha backed away and kept backing until she reached the bedroom door. Then she turned and, with a gasp, opened the door. Then she quickly closed it behind her as she clamped her mouth down on her fist so that he wouldn't hear her cries.

The tears and the agony were for her, not for him.

She meant to keep it that way.

* * *

On Christmas Day, when his children came around, Knowles asked Roland and Cincy to join him alone in the bedroom. He told them he needed to give them something.

They assembled after dinner, seating themselves on the chairs kept around their father's bedside.

Cincy was much older then, and beautiful, like Martha. Her skin was an olive translucence. Her gray eyes, almond in shape, looked kindly out at the world. Still, she was nobody's fool despite the considerable heart she had for the poor community she served with little payment. She had won what Lester required to purchase a lifetime of excellent care after Cincy was gone. She didn't ever ask for any more than that. Now she slid her chair up close beside her father and reached and took his hand in her own. She drew the back of his hand across her cheek. Tears glistened in her eyes.

Roland, the boy with the very dark skin and bright gray eyes like those of his grandfather, Reynaldo Bautista of Makati City, sat silently by while he waited for what his powerful, almost overbearing father, needed to tell them. Roland was still teaching civics in high school and attending sporting events with his sons, ever the happy father.

Like his sister, Cincy, his door was always open to Martha Bautista. Both of them had included her in all family affairs since they had their homes. Their father had requested they do that, and the children had happily obliged him. Which wasn't even that; they loved Martha and were always glad when she came to their homes. Theirs was a special relationship. The children had assumed that connection was the one that ran from their father to Martha. They, in their thoughts about the matter, considered themselves more the beneficiaries of their father's relationship with Martha. It had worked well for everyone concerned. So Roland was at peace that day, though he was anxious for his father's failing health. Still, the children knew this was inevitable.

Sitting at his bedside, in the shadowy afternoon that Christmas Day—while the TV blatted out in the family room and the kids played canasta and cheered on the Bears—, Roland and Cincy, deep within their souls, knew what was coming. How it would be said and what it would mean for their lives was all that was left. Knowles wasted no time.

"I want to tell you that I have lied to you, and that makes me ashamed. It also makes me fearful of the Lord, who I'm about to meet face-to-face. I've made my confession for my sin to Father Tom. His commandment to me was that I make my confession to you. So here it is. Aunt Martha brought you into this world. She is your true birth mother."

He paused, waiting for the sky to fall—or so he imagined.

"I think I've always known that, Dad," Cincy whispered, "but thanks for saying it."

"I've done a bit of research, Dad," Roland said. "The dates of our birth and the date mother died just never did add up. I guessed the reason behind it. But I also guess I never quite admitted it to myself. I chose to believe you more than I chose to believe myself."

"Well said, Ro-Ro," Cincy said, reaching across and squeezing the back of her brother's neck. "Yes, we both chose to believe you, Dad. Looking back, your words were far more important to me than my suspicions. Whatever, we have always loved Martha. She's been included in our lives as much as if this confession had come when we were ten years old. It just doesn't matter now. But, for the record, I forgive you."

"I forgive you too, Father," said Roland. "And like Cincy, I guess I stopped dwelling on all this a long, long time ago. Was Martha aunt or mother? I just never cared which all that much. I loved her either way."

Knowles lay immobile on his back, tears rolling down both sides of his face. He could be heard, suddenly, to be fighting for the next breath.

Realizing what was happening, Cincy stood and leaned down to her father's ear. "We forgive you. We love you. Go on now and be with Mom."

Meaning, Natalia. They weren't going to take that away from him.

And so he passed.

Chapter 38

In late 1944, at Cabanatuan, the Japanese prison camp for Filipinos, Martha Bautista had her breakthrough success. The breakthrough came just two months before American soldiers drove their tanks through the front gates of the camp—Japanese soldiers fleeing into the jungle in all directions—and liberated Martha and the rest of the survivors of the Japanese' years of torture and abuse and starvation. Her success? Martha isolated and cultured Anthrax in her small laboratory. She developed precisely the horrible weapon of mass destruction the Japanese Emperor had commissioned her, and others, to develop.

For the Japanese, however, the development was irrelevant. Irrelevant because, one, the success came too late for the Japanese to mass-produce and weaponize and, two, the success was never announced by Martha, so the Japanese knew nothing about it. To her great credit, within twenty-four hours of liberation at Cabanatuan, Martha had enlisted the help of the Americans in burning down her laboratory, thereby eliminating all manner of cultures and experiments pending, including anthrax. It was over and done, gone, all of her years of work up in smoke.

One aspect of her experiments that did not and never would go up in smoke was the knowledge base Martha had created in culturing anthrax. She left the camp a free woman, accompanied by her child, fathered by one of a hundred rapists, and in possession of the knowledge she knew she would never use.

Never use—at least not until the advent of Richard Dotty in her life.

The story of Martha's anthrax production was only beginning. It had its roots in the murders of the Filipino nurses the night Richard Dotty—himself a deadly organism of mass destruction—visited the dormitory. Because in the bunk above Martha's, the bunk where the young nurse died and was comforted by Martha herself as she was dying, was Martha's daughter, Nettie. She was the daughter raised by Ami but brought to the States by Martha. The young woman went to her death with Martha's words in her ear: "This doesn't end here, my love, for I will avenge you. Then, one day soon, I will join you on the other side, and we will walk hand-in-hand through meadows of heavenly music, and we will dwell by sweet waters for eternity."

Chapter 39

When Michael Gresham's prosecution of Richard Dotty resulted in a mistrial, the judge released Dotty to the benefits of bail. With the aid of his attorney, Mr. Levin, Dotty moved into a cheap hotel on Clark Street, one block off the Loop in downtown Chicago. Dotty's new living situation was reported back to the court in fulfillment of one of the conditions of his release on bail. The reporting document, filed with the court by Attorney Levin was, curiously enough, submitted as a public document that even Martha could access.

Which she did. Now she knew where she could find her daughter's killer.

After the trial, Martha fell into a depression because Michael had let her down. He hadn't killed Dotty—as Martha had counted on, and then he'd blown the murder trial and the killer escaped yet again. But the depression was short-lived when, on the fifth day, she suddenly got angrier than ever before in her life. She left her bed, made it up a final time, and went to work. She would keep her promise to her daughter.

In the next couple of days, she turned her bedroom into a laboratory. Drawing on the knowledge and skill in developing anthrax spore that she had possessed in 1944 Cabanatuan, she successfully grew the spore once again, this time right in her bedroom lab. When she was done, she shut her eyes and said, "Michael, you are set free from your promise to kill Dotty. It was never your problem, to begin with. Forgive me."

She then visited Nettie's grave in Arlington Heights, a place selected for its pastoral, out-of-the-way cemetery, where Martha had committed Nettie until they were together again. It was then time to visit Richard Dotty. Everything else Martha had needed to accomplish was finished.

Only Dotty's existence remained.

Richard Dotty had never seen Martha and knew nothing about what she looked like. The judge had ruled a mistrial before she could testify. During the slaughter itself, Martha had secreted herself beneath her bed and wasn't discovered by Dotty way back then.

So when Martha announced herself—after knocking on Dotty's Door—as a Welcome Wagon caller, and Dotty unbolted his door to see what the old woman wanted, he knew nothing of her real ID.

There she stood, an old woman clinging to a walker, totally non-threatening. She asked to come inside. She said she had gifts for him. She said she had fried chicken. This last part caused the door to open wide, so she shuffled inside.

As the Welcome Wagon did, Martha began passing the small advertising gifts of pens, keychains, coffee cup, and bandages to the new arrival in that part of the city where, Martha explained, it was her job to welcome newcomers.

Richard Dotty had to restrain himself when Martha lifted out of her woven basket the final gift, the ineluctable box lunch, and passed it to the new resident.

"Fried chicken," she nodded at her host. "I made it myself. Please don't open it until after I'm gone or you may have to arm wrestle me for it," Martha joked.

Richard Dotty—anything else, maybe, but never a jokester—told Martha he would keep it sealed until she was gone.

And when her Welcome Wagon basket was empty, and when Martha was making her way out of Dotty's room, she left him with this. "Enjoy your meal, now, but don't share. This is your special gift just to show we love you."

"Well," said Dotty without conviction, "thank you, I guess. I am hungry, and your chicken smells delicious."

Fried chicken: Dotty's favorite meal, at least according to her friend, Marcel Rainford, who knew about such things.

Tears of joy swam into Martha's eyes once she was alone in the hallway outside of Dotty's room. She shuffled mightily for the elevators to make her getaway.

Anthrax would take ten days to do him in. In the meantime, he would be sick beyond anything he'd ever known before. Which would keep him in bed, slowly passing away.

Martha's work was done. After reading about Dotty's demise two weeks later in the *Chicago Tribune*, Martha cleaned up her apartment, disposed of her chemicals and laboratory—no further need—and ate two pieces of the same chicken, a wing, and a drumstick, that she'd gifted to Dotty.

It was time to join Nettie on the beach.

* * *

Michael and Marcel were about to be charged with several crimes when the only witness to the underlying offense died. Without Richard Dotty, there was no proof he had been forced to confess or injured in any way to cause him to confess. Without any illegal confession, there was no subornation of perjury either. There was only Dotty's claim, on the record, true, to Judge Mendoza about the coercion and partial castration. The State's Attorney's Office made the judgment, for many reasons, that no prosecution of Marcel and Michael could ever succeed, so the file was closed.

"Was justice done in the Dotty case?" a CNN reporter asked Michael Gresham.

"Is justice ever done?" Michael was said to have replied.

The video clip of Michael saying this was never run.

Chapter 40

MICHAEL

My family was special to me, but as an American family, it wasn't special at all. There are millions of stories like ours: pull-push, win-lose, enjoy-regret, love-hate (or worse, ignore) and much more. Even more important to me was the certainty I grew up with that I wasn't special. I was just another joe with a family history and a law degree trying to hold his own.

I happened to drop in on Martha the day she died. After there was no answer to my repeated knocking, the landlord let me inside, me being family, where I found her on her bed. She lifted her arms and pulled me toward. her. "I need to tell you about my vision," she whispered.

Here's what she said.

It was a day of green growing leaves and grass and flowers when Martha paid a visit to her daughter. She left the taxicab waiting on the small road just before the cemetery and walked across the sweet-smelling grass, newly mown, to Nettie's resting place.

Up to the grave she crept, slowly sinking to her knees, her left arm extended for balance. Next, she crumpled to the ground just like she always did when visiting Nettie. She closed her eyes and called to her daughter.

The vision began, and she caught sight of her daughter.

The small child, playing just outside the reach of friendly waves swarming ashore on some white sandy beach, was there alone. She looked up at her visitor; Nettie was maybe five. In Martha's hand was a bucket with two children's sand shovels. In her other hand was the book she'd made for the child.

Reaching the shoreline, Martha sat down in the sand and began playfully shoveling sand from the beach to bucket. Seeing this, Nettie turned from her wave-dodging and came to sit with Martha. She accepted the offer of the second sand shovel and, within seconds, was assisting the dreamer in filling the bucket with sand.

This went on for an hour or more until a sand castle was constructed, a sand castle conceived and created by two minds melded as one. When it was complete, Martha and Nettie began a game of tag on the beach. The mother purposely lost each round; that was what mothers do with young children. They then walked hand-in-hand along the beach until coming to a small lean-to where Icees could be purchased. Nettie elected to go for the strawberry flavor; Martha ordered the same. Then they were walking again on the beach, laughing and enjoying their treats even while the sun in the western sky was inching down and down and down. As the sun was disappearing, Martha read briefly from the book before passing it to Nettie. The child hugged her mother, then thanked her for the gift and laughed gaily.

Finally, just before the sun disappeared into the ocean, Nettie stood up from yet another sand castle and looked her mother in the eye. The child was happy and utterly fearless, Martha could see as Nettie turned, her book in hand, and began wading into the water. This time she did not run and dodge the lapping waves but freely—happily—engaged them with her sandy toes as she hiked into deeper and then even deeper water. When she disappeared beneath the surface, Martha's heart filled with joy.

Martha shut her eyes and brushed away her tears. When she opened them again, she was at Nettie's graveside. "Damn it!" she cursed. "I'm still here."

Martha arose and clasped her hands together, eyes closed, lips moving in what? Prayer? Blessing? Exhortation? Watching this from his taxi, the driver's face contorted into a look of concern. His hand touched the door handle but paused when the fare began trudging in the direction of his cab. She climbed into the backseat once again and told the driver she wanted to go home.

Martha returned home and lay down on her bed.

Just before she passed, I asked her about the book she had given Nettie. What was in that book?

She smiled and said, "I told her I'd written the story of her life. It was all right there in the book. 'Had you lived,' I told her, 'here is what you would have known.'"

I held her hand as she took her last, shallow breath. Then Martha was gone.

The loved ones have come onstage then left like a film unwinding. Over the years, I gathered all I could find out about my not-so-special family, and I wrote it all down. I highlighted the parts Martha deserved to know and would have known had history moved over just an inch. When it was all done, I sat down and read what I had. Then, I went out to my car and drove for an hour to the cemetery. After much hiking up and down cemetery rows, I located Nettie's grave.

A clatter of starlings erupted from the trees overhead as I approached.

I told Nettie—who I never knew—hello. Then I stepped across her, over to Martha's grave.

I stooped down and placed this book.

Then I was gone.

THE END

Also by John Ellsworth

THADDEUS MURFEE SERIES

Thaddeus Murfee

The Defendants

Beyond a Reasonable Death

Attorney at Large

Chase, the Bad Baby

Defending Turquoise

The Mental Case

Unspeakable Prayers

The Girl Who Wrote The New York Times Bestseller

The Trial Lawyer (A Small Death)

The Near Death Experience

SISTERS IN LAW SERIES

Frat Party: Sisters In Law

Hellfire: Sisters In Law

MICHAEL GRESHAM SERIES

Lies She Never Told Me

The Lawyer

Secrets Girls Keep

The Law Partners

Carlos the Ant

Sakharov the Bear

Annie's Verdict

Dead Lawyer on Aisle 11

30 Days of Justis

PSYCHOLOGICAL THRILLERS

The Empty Place at the Table

About the Author

[Image: John_EllsworthJune 2016.jpg]

John Ellsworth practiced law while based in Chicago.

For thirty years John defended criminal clients across the United States. He has defended cases ranging from shoplifting to First Degree Murder to RICO to Tax Evasion, and has gone to jury trial on hundreds. His first book, *The Defendants*, was published in January, 2014. John is presently at work on his 24th thriller.

Reception to John's books has been phenomenal; more than 1,000,000 have been downloaded in 40 months. All are Amazon best-sellers. He is an Amazon All-Star every month and is a *USA Today* bestseller.

John Ellsworth lives in Arizona in the mountains and in California on the beach. He has three dogs that ignore him but worship his wife, and bark day and night until another home must be abandoned in yet another move.

johnellsworthbooks.com
johnellsworthbooks@gmail.com

Email Signup

If you would like to be notified of new book publications, please sign up for my email list. You will receive news of new books, newsletters, and occasional drawings for prizes.

— John Ellsworth

Made in the USA
Columbia, SC
02 December 2019

84221797R00121